DANGEROUS LEDGES

Fallon Raynes

Dangerous Ledges

This work of fiction is from the author's imagination. Anything in this book resembling a person, living or dead, or any events/displays, public or private, is purely coincidence. Trying to map out all the locations listed in this book may cause dismay, irritation, frustration and insanity. Please refrain from contacting any online map company to lodge complaints.

Edited by: Janet Fix (thewordverve.com)
Cover Design by: Joshua Jadon
Barn Photo Credit: BJ Holwerda – bjholwerda on Instagram
Interior Design by Bob Houston eBook Formatting

ISBN: 978-1-7344649-0-0 eBook
ISBN: 978-1-7344649-1-7 Paperback
ISBN: 978-1-7344649-2-4 Hardcover

Library of Congress Control Number: 2020902788

Author's Website: https://www.fallonraynes.com/

To My Beautiful Daughter,

God blessed me the day you finally decided to enter the world. You are my light, and my life. I pray the man you married keeps you safe, loved, and happy. I pray you do the same for him in return. I Love You Always. <3 <3

***

To all the loved ones that God handpicked from this earth, while I was crawling my way toward becoming a published author. You were loved and are deeply missed. I pray we can all meet again someday. -- MH, RH, EH, PH, LB, BD, BD

Chapter 1

Saturday – Late October

His long legs reached the door first, slamming the heavy barrier in her face. He locked it from the other side. He would not lose this time. One way or another, she'd come around to his way of thinking.

She banged her fists against the wooden door and shouted, "Ledge, you crazy bastard! Let me out! Why are you doing this?"

Ledge laughed. "You're mine, Lizabeth! You don't get to leave me like you did!" *Never again will you leave me. I'll never let you go.*

She would not escape easily. There were no windows, and the lathe-and-plaster walls were not easy to punch a fist through. *I love old houses*, he thought. No one was around to hear her screams and commotion out in these middle-of-nowhere Michigan woods. *Besides, she won't continue much longer—she might break a nail.*

He walked down the hall to the kitchen, his stomach growling. "Time for something to eat."

As he grilled a PB&J, he noticed she had stopped beating on the door. He sighed in relief that she'd calmed down. He picked up his sandwich and took a bite, plotting his next move. He knew what he had to do, but he wasn't sure when he wanted to take action. Morning would shed light on that subject, pending his caged little tiger's mood. She had always been a little spitfire. He loved that about her. He'd misjudged the dose he'd used to knock her out and was thankful that he'd been able to place her petite body on the couch before she came to. "Your plan is in motion, Ledge, ol' boy."

***

She looked around the room. Anxiety attack over, she breathed heavily, concentrating on trying to regain a steady pattern. *No sense in crying. It won't do any good. You have to think.*

"Hard to do with a headache, Liza," she whispered to herself. What had he given her? Her recollection of how she had come to be in this room was fuzzy.

She had a bandage on her right hand, which was throbbing. Glass. She remembered broken glass on the floor. She closed her brown eyes, pulled the ponytail holder from her long brown hair, and clutched the sides of her head to massage her temples. After a few minutes, she opened her eyes and searched the small room.

There was a shabby old couch, a matching throw pillow, a blanket, and a bucket.

Wait! A bucket?

She walked over to it on unsteady legs. She'd seen those buckets before in a sporting-goods store. *Oh. My. God.* Shaking her head, she realized she might be trapped in this room for quite a while—because right next to the bucket was a roll of toilet paper. Bile rose in her throat as she shut down her anger. Being angry would not help her. She focused again on her breathing. *Think!*

Walking around the room, this time she noticed a cooler behind the couch, which she opened. There were bottles of water and a few apples. Sighing, she looked around again. Other than those few items, there was nothing else in the claustrophobic closet of a room—with no windows. Not a one. The carpeting was a horrendous burnt-orange color and well worn. She wondered how old the house was. At least the room had a light switch that worked, and she flicked it on and off a few times.

She figured the room had once had at least one window. Probably had been a small bedroom at one time. Tapping the walls, she could not find the studs. Everything sounded the same. *Darn it. Lathe-and-plaster walls. I will find that window.*

She walked to the thick wooden door and rested her back against it. She listened closely but didn't hear anything. The place was like a vault.

Thinking back to her high-school drafting classes, she recalled the plans she used to draw. Visualizing what a typical house would look like, she walked forward to the opposite wall. *If this room was a bedroom at one time, and the door is behind me, this wall in front of me should have a window.*

She snapped her head around when she heard him humming outside the door. Rushing over to the couch, she sat down quickly while he unlocked the door. The smell of a grilled sandwich filled the room as he slid the tray along the floor with one of those reacher-handle things she'd seen on TV. She snickered, despite her worries. He was such an idiot. She wondered if she could have taken him by surprise, but didn't see a way. He had the upper hand for now.

"There you go, Lizabeth. Just like I used to make for you when we were married. Enjoy!"

"Bastard!" she hissed. It was all she could think to say.

"Ah, I've so missed your sweet-nothings." Pulling his long, handsome face into a smirk, he quickly ducked his towering frame out of view and locked the door again.

On cue, her stomach rumbled. She studied the tray of Lay's potato chips and the grilled PB&J. Despite her hunger, she couldn't bring herself to eat the food in front of her. He could have poisoned it, whatever. The simple fact that he'd made it was enough to make her gag.

Stomach growling again, she admitted that it was better to keep herself fueled. She doubted that he'd poisoned it—not so early in the game, anyway. *And what game was he playing?* She picked up the tray and sat down on the couch. Pulling apart the sandwich, she burned her finger on the dripping jelly. She cursed him and then more delicately probed the sandwich for anything suspicious. With a shrug of her shoulders—*to heck with it*—she put the sandwich back together and took a bite.

***

Turning from the door, he stalked back to the kitchen to clean up the mess from lunch. He couldn't trust her enough to ask her to do it. The thought made him irritable, so he pushed it out of his head. She really looked great since their divorce. Cheerleader curves back to where they were. Should have divorced her three years ago if he could have known she'd get her body back as a result. He shook his head. Again, his mind was taking him places he didn't want to go.

Time was on his side. Everyone thought she was in the Caribbean, relaxing and loving life. Yes, he had time. Smiling, he placed the clean dishes in the rack to dry. After wiping the counter, he quietly walked down the hall and heard small thudding noises. *Let her bang all she wants. She won't find a way out.*

Now whistling, he placed the dishrag on the sink to dry and headed to the back porch to watch the sunset. One of the relaxation techniques he'd learned from the doctor, who'd said, "Find something to focus on that brings you peace."

Have to stay focused and keep the demons at bay. So many colors across the sky tonight. She would love this sunset. Lizabeth had enjoyed the back-porch swing his dad had put in for his mom at their home. It had always relaxed Ledge, to hold Lizabeth's small frame in his strong arms as he gently rocked that swing. *I need to put a swing out here, too, if my plan works.* Whistling to himself, he picked up his stress ball and squeezed, squeezed, squeezed as a sense of calm washed over him.

Chapter 2

Knock, knock, tap, tap, knock. Nothing. Not ready to give up, she listened again for any sound outside of the door, then she started over on the wall across from the door. She had traversed the room and found an old nail lying on the floor. She used that as her marker. Her hand was getting sore from pounding the nail into the various places on the walls. She had marked the last row she tried and decided to go up from there about five inches. Thankfully, he wouldn't notice the marks easily, with the walls being in such a state of disrepair. The wallpaper was peeling in quite a few spots, and the old pattern of flowers covered the nail holes well.

She took a moment to rest and caught herself chewing on her freshly painted fingernails—done up in a Caribbean nail pattern especially for the trip. She sighed. Money down the drain.

It had started out in her savings account to go toward a surprise "honeymoon" for her and Ledge's anniversary this year. She had worked her tail off on a major project for almost two years and received a big bonus for her efforts. She had wanted to make it up to him for all her overtime. Frowning, her eyes focused on the wall as her mind replayed memories of the day that changed her plans, her life...

***

Caught in the Act
Early May

He sputtered, "Holy fuck! What are you— It's... it's not what it looks like."

"Oh, really? What do you expect me to think when I see my husband with his pants down around his ankles and a naked blonde bent over his desk?"

"Liza, I—" Ledge didn't finish the sentence as he struggled to pull up his drawers.

"Shut up! Save your lies! You've been lying to me for so many years... they're wasted on me." She saw the realization in his eyes; she had already suspected he was cheating again. "Yes, I know all about the marriedmen.com site and saw the profile you made."

Meanwhile, the blonde was trying to move as quickly as possible to gather her clothes and make an exit.

"Umm..." Liza held up her hand, eyebrow raised, and blocked the doorway. "Sorry, Blondie. I have something to say to you. I don't care if he's paying you or if you think fucking a married man is fun, but karma is a bitch. When you catch the man you love with another woman under him, remember today, and you'll know exactly how I feel at this very minute."

Vibrating with anger and hurt, she heard Ledge start to speak and whipped around to cut him off. "You cheating bastard! You don't get to do this to me anymore."

She walked out of his office on shaky legs with as much grace as she could muster, leaving the dumbfounded cheats behind. Reaching her truck, she slid into the seat, slammed the door, and finally let the tears fall. *This will be the last time he hurts me.* No amount of information from the PI could have prepared her for the scene she'd just witnessed. With a deep breath, she wiped her tears and headed home. The last thing she wanted was for him to see her crying.

***

After quickly packing the rest of her belongings that she hadn't had time to pack before she'd caught him in the act, she pressed the reset-to-factory-settings button on her phone. While she watched it erase everything left on the phone that she hadn't already removed, she murmured to herself, "I wish I could do that with all my memories of him." Liza pulled the house key off her key ring and placed it on the counter next to the cell phone and her wedding ring. "I won't need those anymore."

She brushed her hands together, satisfied. There would be no way for him to hound her while she tried to re-bundle the pieces of her life. Divorce wasn't desirable, but sometimes there was no other answer. Taking one last look around the house to ensure she had everything she wanted to take, she drew a deep breath and let it out slowly as she turned to leave for good. All the memories, all the projects, all that time... wasted. Packing had kept her focused. With that done, the tears threatened to spill again. Pulling a tissue from her pocket, she wiped them away.

Liza locked the front door on her way to her shiny white truck she had purchased in anticipation of this day. The day she had dreaded. She put the truck in gear, slowly pulled out of the drive with the trailer shadowing her, and didn't look back. Referencing her mental to-do list, she checked off a few things:

- Catch Cheating Bastard - Check
- Leave Cheating Bastard - Check
- Get moved into a new place - On my way now
- Call a good divorce attorney - Dialing now
- RESET LIFE – Working on it.

***

A Week Later at Liza's Office

"Hello, I have a delivery for a Lizabeth McAllister."

"That's me."

Smiling, the deliveryman handed her the flowers. "Have a nice day," he said and tipped his nonexistent hat. Before she even read the card, Liza's hackles were up. She glanced at Ann, their receptionist, who had quirked her eye up in question. Liza ignored it and excused herself. She made it back to her office and set the flowers on her desk as she looked at the card—from guess who?

I'm very sorry. I miss you. Please call me.

She tossed the card on her desk, pushed the flowers to the farthest corner, reining in her need to smash them against the wall. Trying to brush off her anger, Liza called her best friend, Trinity Gold. "I need to talk."

They wasted no time in making plans to meet at Trinity's house that evening.

*****

Trinity's mouth dropped open, her expression one of shock. "He really signed it that way? 'Love, Cheating Bastard'?"

They were sitting in the Golds' living room, each in a comfortable chair, wrapped in a blanket, with a hot drink nearby—tea for Trinity and cocoa for Liza.

"No. I added that part."

Trinity put a hand to her heart. "Oh, goodness. You had me there. But he might as well have written it." She sniffed and took a sip of her tea.

The drama queen. Liza's best friend. And Liza loved every bit of her. Especially during times like these.

"Yeah, that's my automatic response whenever I think of him." With her face coiled in disgust, Liza reached for her hot cocoa on the coffee table, being careful not to spill it on herself or Trinity's furniture. "When does Oliver get home? Am I imposing?"

"Not for another hour or so. He's helping a friend move a new refrigerator into his man cave. And, thankfully, Abbie is spending the night at a friend's house tonight. The last time those twelve-year-old girls got together over here, it was after two in the morning before I finally stopped hearing the giggles coming from her bedroom."

Liza laughed, knowing full well how much Trinity loved her family and being a mother. Abbie was a sweet child and was definitely going to be a heartbreaker with her blond curls and eyes of the brightest blue. She was already attracting attention from the boys, Trinity had told her recently. Ollie was certainly going to have his hands full trying to keep the guys off their lawn.

Trinity adjusted the blanket that covered her lap and cleared her throat before saying, "Uh, are you sure you don't want to talk to him?"

"Hell to the NO! You must still be a sucker for his hot looks. Hmm?" Liza gave her friend a teasing smirk. "Believe me, he's not the same tall, dark, and handsome football player we used to cheer for, the guy I fell in love with. I have *zero* desire to be with a repetitive cheater and liar and general jerk. It's not easy walking around town, looking at every pretty young face, thinking he may have slept with her too. It makes me sick every time I think about it."

Trinity frowned. "I've noticed you've lost some weight since—" she flailed her hands "—you found out he was back to his cheating ways."

Liza shrugged. "A bit, I guess. I've had a lot on my mind, for obvious reasons. And now this, of course."

"I get it. I do." Trinity tilted her head as her expression softened. "So, what did you do with the flowers?"

"I took them to the nursing home and asked if anyone there was having a bad day and could use a bouquet. I made the old gal cry when I took them to her room, but at least those were tears of happiness."

"Best thing to do."

"Yeah, I was glad they did someone some good. I cringe now when I think back, because flowers were his go-to move when he was feeling bad about something he'd done. I don't want or need anything that reminds me of him. It'll be hard enough facing the twins when I go see them this week at college. I'll have to explain the divorce then."

"So, Ledge hasn't mentioned anything to them, huh? You would have heard something."

"He's probably hoping it will all go away. It's just as well; the twins are finishing up their spring finals. They stay at the dorms to keep the distractions to a minimum, so they won't notice I've left the house."

There was silence between them as Liza's mind whirled, and Trinity waited to jump in as needed. Liza had never felt more fortunate for their friendship than at that very moment. Trinity knew some of the sad stories of Liza's life with Ledge, but mostly, Liza had tried to keep things to herself... because she wanted to believe it wasn't so.

Now, though, she was ready to spill her guts. "Looking back on all those times I'd *thought* he was cheating ... well, I was right all along. All that trying to 'better himself' bullshit, quitting smoking so he could 'live longer for me and the kids.' Ha! I went through hell while he was on that mind-altering drug, Cantril."

"Yeah, I remember you mentioning it every now and then."

"It totally messed him up as far as having control over his emotions. Zero to crazy in less than one second. He did quit smoking. I'll give him that. But he didn't quit *boinking*. I found out his online dating profile was started over two years ago! And then the naked blonde on his desk." Liza grabbed at her hair and yanked from frustration as she bent forward and put her elbows on her knees. "She had to know he was married. I mean, our pictures are right there in his office! How does a woman do something like that, knowing he's married?"

"I honestly don't understand that, either. The whole thing is so trashy." Trinity waved her hand in the air and wrinkled her nose, as if trying to push away a nasty smell. "So, you haven't actually spoken with him since, uh, you caught him with his pants down?"

"No, and quite frankly, I'm surprised he hasn't tried to show up at my office. I think he knows he won't be welcome there, and unless he's tried to follow me home, he doesn't know where I'm staying yet. So far, so good! I don't need to see him again until the day in court when the divorce will be final."

"How much longer?"

"About a month, the attorney said, unless Ledge contests what we've proposed. And he shouldn't protest, since I don't want anything from that house. I've taken what belongs to me, and that's all I want. The house was his parents' before their accident, and it never really felt like ours when I moved in. Anyway, my attorney isn't very happy because we have the proof to go for more, but I don't want it to drag on like the brutal divorce Chrissie went through. I want to be done with him." Chrissie was another cherished friend from their group.

"You think he's received the papers yet?"

"I haven't heard. They were supposed to call me after he was served. I told him I was done this time, so it shouldn't shock him too much."

"Well, I'm sure that will let him know how serious you are. I'm surprised he hasn't found you and tried to make up, like he did last year. He hid his craziness from Ollie and me very well, I have to say. I had no idea he had gone berserk and tried to hurt you. I'm sorry you had to go through all that, Liza. What a freaking nightmare."

"Nothing either of you could have done. It got scary a few times, but he regained his self-control before anything physical happened. The verbal part was hard enough to handle. The words still ring in my ears. I'd told him that the next time he went off on me, I was gone. I guess he figured if he didn't get angry, he could get away with cheating instead, and I would never find out. Hard not to think something's going on when he comes home from work and immediately takes a shower before heading to the den to watch TV." Liza set her drink down on the table and rewrapped herself in the blanket. She shuddered and said, "Darn, Trin. Just because its spring doesn't mean it's warm. Are you going to turn your heat back on?"

Laughing at her friend, Trinity grabbed the cups off the table and headed for the kitchen. "You don't pay our bills, woman. This has to last, and unless it drops below forty degrees outside, it stays off. Besides, I sleep better when it's cooler in the house." She stuck her tongue out at Liza as she walked to the kitchen.

Glancing around the living room, Liza noticed a photo of the two couples—she and Ledge, Trinity and Oliver—taken during the New Year's party they'd attended this year.

She sighed, a little bit of jealousy creeping in. Trin and Ollie had been inseparable in high school and still were. The "Ledge and Liza" in that picture used to be the same way. Staring at the New Year's photo, Liza looked at it for the first time with a clearer vision. It was a farce. Ledge had already been cheating long before that night. Liza's backtracking had led her to that conclusion, which pushed her to hire a private investigator to ferret out the truth. Liza turned away from that memory.

Tears threatened again, and she wiped them away before Trin entered the living room with a heaping bowl of Liza's favorite ice cream: Chocolate Overload. Trin sure knew how to make her feel better. Smiling, Liza accepted the bowl and dug in before Trin had a chance to sit down. With her short legs curled beneath her and the blanket in place, Trinity asked the hard question, something Liza suspected her friend had wanted to know for a long time. "I know it's none of my business, and you can tell me to fuck off, but how many times has he cheated on you?"

Liza set her bowl down on the coffee table as the slow burn started at the pit of her stomach. No longer interested in her favorite indulgence, she formed her words before speaking. Humiliation washed across her face as Trin watched her.

"It was about a year and a half after we were married. One night, after we had a great night out dancing and laughing like we hadn't in a few months, he told me. Ledge blurted it out in such a rush that I hadn't time to absorb the words. He must have felt guilty. Said he would never do it again if I'd forgive him. It was with someone he worked with. He said it was because she came on to him, and he couldn't understand why and wanted to find out." Liza sighed, gathered her composure, and continued.

"When I told him I was not going to stop him from seeing her, he didn't know what to say. I knew if he wasn't going to be faithful then… well, I wasn't going to have a marriage with him. I told him so in no uncertain terms. It was like it flipped a switch in him, Trin. He stopped seeing her, started courting me again, and then the woman ended up moving away shortly after. I guess she couldn't take the embarrassment at work. Things were very good between us after that. I still kept an eye on things, though, because I figured, for sure, he would do it again, but he never strayed—at least not until sometime in the past few years. Of course, what do I really know? He could have strayed… I don't know, a hundred times."

Unchecked tears ran down Liza's face as she spoke, and Trinity's eyes were brimming as well. Trinity left the chair and wrapped her arms around her best friend. "Just let it out."

And Liza bawled like a baby.

Chapter 3

July

Oliver kissed Trinity goodbye at the door and winked at her, "Don't stay out all night."

"We won't, dear. We're going to celebrate Liza's divorce and see if we can't talk her into the cruise that Chrissie mentioned. Love you." Blowing a kiss to Ollie, she turned toward the waiting car and waved ecstatically at her two girlfriends. Happy whoops of laughter came from the Chrissie's new bright-red Mustang convertible. Chrissie had recently leased it, thanks to her recent job working for a cruise line in the Caribbean as one of the evening singers. She had a set of pipes on her, which had always come in handy when they were on the cheer squad together back in high school.

Everyone had referred to them as "the Triplets." Even though they didn't look alike, they were always together. Chrissie and Trinity were two of the fliers in the group. Both had the petite frame and build. They would spin off from the top of the small human pyramids and land on their feet. Liza stayed on the ground, although she had been up there with them at one time; she'd fallen and severely sprained her ankle during a practice in their sophomore year. That injury had kept her on the ground for the remainder of high school—per doctor's orders. Liza still knew when a storm was coming because her ankle burned and throbbed.

Climbing into the back seat, Trinity set her purse down, leaned forward, and hugged her friends. It felt so good to be going out again with them, even if it was only for one night.

"Thank you so much for this, ladies. I feel like we're back in high school again," Liza said, her primo smile making a return appearance. Trinity had missed that smile.

"I think I can speak for Chrissie, too, when I say 'I concur.'" Trinity laughed and looked at Chrissie to confirm she was spot-on with that statement. Chrissie gave her the thumbs-up and backed out the driveway.

"Let's hit it, girls!" Chrissie declared as she shifted and then floored it.

Cheers and laughter filled the car. The Triplets were at it again.

***

Liza brought the shots back to the table without spilling a drop in the cramped bar. "You girls ready to go find a quieter bar?"

Laughter spilled out of Chrissie. "Are you getting old on us?"

"I must be!" Downing her shot, she eyed Trinity, who swallowed hers equally as fast.

"Let's get out of here. I think I've lost my hearing," Trinity hollered over the thumping speakers, making a face at Chrissie.

"What?" Liza yelled with her hand cupped around her ear, smirking at Chrissie, then sticking her tongue out, poking fun at her.

"Ha-ha!" Chrissie yelled over the bass.

As they grabbed their coats and headed for the door, a handsy tall man grabbed Chrissie's arm and asked her to dance. She politely declined and tried to wriggle free of his grasp. But he wouldn't let go. Trinity saw this and tugged on Liza's coat—she was almost to the door—and gestured toward Chrissie, who was still struggling to get away from the obviously drunken man.

"What the heck...?" Liza said as Trinity walked straight up to the man.

"Please release my friend. Now!" she said.

By this time, the bouncer had caught sight of the commotion and was making his way toward them. Liza was now standing next to her friends and repeated Trinity's request, adding, "You don't want any trouble, do you? Let her be."

The hulking drunk man looked at Liza. "Buzz off! We're goin' to *daaance,*" he slurred.

"I warned you," Liza said and stomped her heeled foot onto the top of the big guy's shoe. Howling, he bent over, releasing Chrissie's arm in the process. As Chrissie backed away, Liza went in for the "kill," punching the man straight in the nose. Perfect hit.

The girls made a beeline for the door just as the bouncer arrived, leaving him to deal with the pushy guy, who was cursing and hollering as he held his nose and bounced up and down on one leg.

"OMG!" Chrissie yelled. "That was crazy!"

"Get to the car!" Trinity hollered, and grabbed Liza's hand to pull her along.

"Oh my God!" Chrissie said again, as she put the car in gear. "I haven't been ambushed like that in a long time. Thank you, ladies!"

From the back seat, Trinity shouted, "The Triplets are BACK!"

They decided to head to the Back Door Saloon, located a few miles out of town. A much more low-key establishment, with mostly laidback country folk for customers, out to drink beer and listen to good live country music.

Once they'd settled in and ordered their beers, Chrissie and Trinity finally stared Liza down.

She stared back. "What? The Hulk had it coming."

"We're really surprised you did that." Trinity looked at Chrissie to chime in.

She said, "Yeah, not like you. But, hey, it worked."

Shrugging, Liza said, "Eh. I've taken some defense classes. Ledge scared the crap out of me, and I didn't want to get a gun."

Astounded, her friends' jaws dropped to the table. Trinity recovered first. "Why didn't you tell us it was that bad?"

"Why? What would you have done? It wasn't bad enough for me to leave him, and he snapped out of it before he tried to hurt me. But it was spacey the way he used to look at me, like he was staring straight through me or didn't even know who I was. It was like he was filled with blind fury and..." She paused, shook her head. "When the next day came around, he'd ask me what had happened the night before. I was always dumbfounded that he didn't remember. Then, when I'd tell him about his rage and how I thought he was going to hit me... well, he was shocked. Even a little scared himself. He couldn't recall anything after supper that first night it happened. That's when I begged him to go off that Cantril. It was screwing with his head.

When they researched the drug, there were many reviews about the drug and its side effects, including depression and psychotic and rage-fueled episodes. However, there were people who'd had excellent success with it, so he took it. He apologized all over himself that first night, and every time after that. I felt for him, but it didn't stop. In fact, it was merely a week after that incident that I showed up at your door, Trinity—that was last fall, remember? That night, he threw a glass vase of flowers at me. I grabbed my keys and ran."

"I remember, but I didn't know it wasn't the first time."

Chrissie's expression was filled with concern. "Hey, why didn't either of you tell me this was going on?"

The waitress approached with the beers, and Liza handed her a twenty, then turned back to Chrissie. "Your divorce from William was almost over, and you didn't need my stress added to yours. I'm really thankful the kids were already at college by then. I don't know how I would have handled it if they'd been at home."

Chrissie shook her head and smiled a weak smile. "I'm sorry I was a basket case. Thank you both for taking care of me during that time. You're my rocks."

Trinity took a big sip of her beer, then smacked her hands on the table. "All right. Enough of this downer talk. Let's hit the dance floor. We have some energy to burn." She pulled her friends up from their chairs and dragged them to the dance floor. They danced until a slow song came on and then dropped themselves back into their chairs. After chugging the rest of their first round of beers, they immediately ordered another round.

"Chrissie, why don't you tell Liza about your new plan?"

"Well, I was hoping, Liza, you would come on that cruise you've been trying to plan the past year. I know you wanted to surprise Ledge and take him, but why not treat yourself? I sing at night, so I can spend all day with you, and you can come to my shows and... well, maybe you'll even meet someone." Chrissie waggled her eyebrows at Liza.

Liza's face morphed into a variety of expressions as she thought about it—from *I don't think so*, to *Maybe*, to finally a bright smile. "Yes, I like that idea!" She leaned over and hugged Chrissie. "I like that idea very much. Thank you! What about you, Trinity? You think you can come, too?"

Shaking her head, she said, "Definitely not. Ollie would totally balk at that idea. Plus, he has a cruise planned for us after Abbie goes off to college." She waved her hand in the air. "Anyway, you'll have just as much fun without me there. Chrissie gave me the rundown of all the activities you can choose from, on the ship and at the islands. Besides, she'll be there to do stuff during the day with you."

Chrissie held up her hand toward Liza for a high-five. Liza smacked it and grinned.

"We'll have fun!" Chrissie said. "You'll see. I'll send you a couple cruise dates, and you can pick which one you want. I'll also email you the links to the islands, and you can pick what you want to do. You know me... I'm up for anything." She gave an exaggerated wink.

Liza giggled. "Okay. Sounds like a plan. We're on."

Trinity squealed with delight. "Oooo, I'm so happy to hear this."

Liza lifted her beer and toasted, "To my best friends. You girls sure know how to make me feel better. Thank you. I've missed this."

"Group hug!" Chrissie said, standing with her arms spread out wide.

After the hug, Trinity dragged them to the dance floor once again.

Chapter 4

Taking a break Monday afternoon at work, Liza opened the email she had received from Chrissie earlier that morning. It included a link to the cruise line with two departure dates in October, both of which were times when Chrissie would be performing in the evenings and available during the day.

This was perfect for Liza. It gave her plenty of time to plan for her vacation, since it was still several months away. And October was slower for her workwise.

She scrolled down and noted that it was a seven-day cruise. Boarding at San Juan and traveling to St. Thomas, Barbados, St. Lucia, St. Kitts, St. Maarten, and ending back at San Juan. Chrissie had also included the links to a few hotels she recommended and a list of attractions for all the islands on the cruise route. Liza made a note to herself to arrange for a flight to San Juan.

She was reviewing the activities on the islands—many of which seemed very similar to each other—when there was a knock at the door. "Come in."

Ann entered the office with a dozen lavender roses in hand and set them on Liza's desk corner. Liza started to reach for them to find a card.

"You won't find a card. It arrived a few minutes ago, and the delivery man said the sender wished to remain anonymous."

"Well, that's odd. I bet Chrissie or Trinity set this up to surprise me. How's your day so far, Ann?"

"Well, no flowers for me, but all is well and quiet up front today. I'll welcome that, for a Monday." She smiled and left the room, leaving Liza pondering who had sent the roses.

"I really hope they're from one the girls," she muttered to herself. She grabbed her phone and sent a group text to the girls, asking about the flowers.

It wasn't her birthday. Glancing at the calendar, she then realized the significance of this particular date. Her phone buzzed, and she didn't even have to look to know that Trin and Chris had not sent the flowers. A chill crawled up her arms.

Today was their wedding anniversary. She'd had lavender roses in her bouquet. Ledge was the anonymous sender. He hadn't made any attempt to talk to her since the last bouquet of flowers he'd sent with the halfhearted apology. They signed the papers last week—not a peep from him in the courtroom that day, not a glance her way. Until today. Of course he would today. He'd lost his mind.

Uneasiness plagued her for the rest of the afternoon. She told no one. On her way home, she deposited the roses at the same nursing home where she had taken the previous unwelcome gift of flowers a few months ago. Still on edge, she kept checking her rearview mirror as she made her way home in evening traffic.

***

After taking a long, hot shower, Liza felt a little bit better. The chill was washed away, and she was now planted in a comfy chair on her back porch, her feet tucked beneath her. She had her laptop on her lap, with a notepad and daily planner next to her. Feeling even more empowered to take that cruise, Liza reopened Chrissie's email. She opened her planner to October. Since it was still a ways off, the entire month was blank. Her kids would have already started back for their second year at college. There was nothing holding her back. Smiling, she chose the first October date Chris had mentioned and penciled it in. That would have her back before month-end duties. The cruise left on Sunday, so she made a note to take off work the Friday before, to get packed and rested, ready to fly to San Juan for boarding the ship.

She then clicked on the links to the hotels in San Juan, considering their amenities and proximity to the ship. She really liked the looks of the Olive Boutique. It wasn't far from the dock where she'd board. She wrote that down and started an email draft to Chrissie with her notes about the cruise date and hotel she'd selected.

Next, she opened the list of attractions and activities. She took her time going through the options, jotting down the ones that jazzed her the most, including details for each.

She then opened a new spreadsheet on her laptop. Being a consultant for Midland Consulting Firm, she was efficient with putting budgets together for clients and organizing her to-do lists with spreadsheets. *The cruise definitely needs a spreadsheet*, she thought as she started filling in the data. She even splurged on a grand suite with an extended balcony. She'd saved plenty for this trip—over ten grand—and decided to do it in high style.

But when she saw the so-far total, she about choked. She was already close to two thousand dollars, and that was only the cruise reservation. The miser in her whispered in her ear, *"You mustn't. You can't. This is totally out of character."* As she was about to delete the information and start over, she let her mouse hover over the spreadsheet. After all, the reservation itself was a reduced priced because it was a "fill the ship" deal. So, she was saving money right there.

Finally, she said, "Just do it!"

And she did. She added in the hotel, parking fees at the airport, food, new clothing ... any miscellaneous expense she could think of, no matter how small. She was generous to herself, not holding back, but still frugal when frugality was warranted. She'd take twelve days off work, including some days before and after for prep and regroup time.

When she had all items included to her satisfaction, she sat back, closed her eyes for a moment, and said a little prayer. Slowly opening her right eye, she looked at the grand total of all the expenses. Then she opened her left eye, a mixture of relief and excitement flowing through her. Her ten-grand budget was near perfect had Ledge been going with her. Rounding up to the nearest hundred, her total as a single, pampered traveler came to forty-three hundred—on the high side even.

Releasing the air from her lungs that she hadn't realized she was holding, she looked toward the sky at the tops of the trees. They barely held the sun. Her stomach growled at that moment. Time to eat.

Carefully stretching, so as not to drop her laptop, she finished her email to Chrissie:

Chrissie,

I finished the cruise itinerary, and here is everything I have planned. Let me know if this doesn't work for you. Call me so we can go over everything one last time before I book. I decided on leaving the third week in October, the first date you mentioned, so I can be back before November.

I'd like to book everything within a few days so the prices don't go up. You know me and money. Lol. Attached is my spreadsheet that includes the various activities that interest me the most, including costs (I know you're doubling over with laughter) ... but we don't have to do everything. Whatever works best for you, too. Let's talk soon. Much love! L

She hit send, took in a deep breath and let it out, satisfied with her progress. Before she could even gather her notepad and close her laptop, her email pinged. Chrissie had already replied:

Looks Great! Can't wait! Get this BOOKED NOW!!!!! :-D

Liza shook her head and smirked. Chrissie was so "seat-of-her-pants." Picking up her phone, she sent Chris a text:

Are you sure? Did you even look at the whole email?

YES! Get it BOOKED NOW!

OKAY! STOP YELLING! Lol.

Liza's stomach growled again, but she ignored it. Feeling energized by Chris's lively text, she opened the link to the cruise line and booked her cruise dates. She did the same with the flight and the hotel. The basics were now done. She could deal with the activities on the islands later. Her stomach was not going to be ignored. The sun had set, and she was starting to get a headache from lack of food and light on the porch. Grabbing her laptop, notepad, and planner, she headed inside, in search of food.

***

Liza didn't hear the movement in the backyard shrubs as she walked into the house, forgetting to lock the kitchen door behind her.

Chapter 5

Sunday - Present Day

Morning dawned upon Ledge's face. Sprinkles of dust floated in the air as he gathered his thoughts. Resting his head on his left arm, he recalled how beautiful Lizabeth looked first thing in the morning. The morning sun would caress her bare shoulders—she always slept naked when they were first married. She had told him it was to entice him to touch her anytime. Truth was, they couldn't keep their hands off each other. Their mutual attraction had been as powerful as the Niagara Falls, where they had honeymooned. Although Lizabeth loved seeing the falls, listening to the roar of the tumultuous waters, most of the trip had been spent between the sheets.

They'd both wanted children—especially Lizabeth, who had been an only child. She wanted as many kids as she could have, she'd once joked. He was not one to deny her any wish. He smiled, thinking back on that conversation. He, too, wanted many kids. He had lost his older brother to a boating accident when he was only eight. Then, his parents were killed by a drunk driver at the start of his freshman year of high school. His only living relative was his mother's mom, Gram Ledges, his namesake. After his parents died, she'd moved into their home and took care of him, so that he wouldn't have to move.

Jostled from his reminiscing, Ledge heard the insistent knocking. *Lizabeth.* His room was right next to hers. He roused and headed for the bathroom. *After all, she's not going anywhere.*

Ledge quickly moved through his morning routine, starting with a hot shower. He had transformed the old claw-foot bathtub so he could use it as a shower as well—with a roundabout curtain and pipes running up the cupboard at the end of the tub to hold the showerhead.

After he'd dried off and wrapped the towel around his waist, he stood in front of the mirror and wiped away the steam so he could assess his whiskers. Grabbing the razor and shaving cream, he stopped and stared at his reflection. His neatly trimmed, dark hair was showing grey on the sides. His chin was a bit scruffy. Lizabeth loved it when he went a little haggard sometimes. He nixed the idea of shaving; he put everything down, scratched his chin, and brushed his teeth. He pulled the towel from his waist, hung it on the back of the bathroom door, and walked across the hall to his bedroom. He dressed for comfort in blue jeans, a soft denim, button-up shirt, and his Nikes. He caught himself in the mirror above the dresser and grinned. "Time to pour on the charm, Ledge, ol' boy. Let's go see what mood my Liza-bear is in."

***

Her mind whirled with questions the minute she opened her eyes. *How did he get into my house? How did I not hear him come in? Where the hell am I? Why did he bring me here? What is that crazy bastard up to?* She replayed the words he'd said yesterday: "You're mine, Lizabeth! You don't get to leave me like you did!" *What am I in for? Why did he wait until now to kidnap me? Why didn't he do it earlier, before the divorce was final? If he wanted to kill me, he could have done it when we were married, claimed the life insurance. No, he doesn't need money. His business does well, and his family left him quite a trust fund. So, why am I here?*

Then, she realized the answers to those questions mattered very little to her at the moment. She was more determined than ever to find that window and get the hell out of there. *Soon. Very soon.*

At least she had managed to catch a few winks, even on the lumpy, old, smelly couch. Liza methodically tapped the nail into the wall again, when she heard the key in the lock. Rushing to the couch, she pushed the nail between the cushions. She cursed herself for missing the opportunity to catch him at the door, to push her way past him and run for her life. It was her alternative escape plan, should she not be able to find the window.

"Rise and shine, Liza-bear."

She gave him a steely glare as he entered the room and closed the door behind him, blocking it with his body. "What would you like for breakfast this beautiful morning?"

"Beautiful is it? I wouldn't know. I have no view." Liza sneered sarcastically.

Her sour note did nothing to faze him. "Yes, the sun has risen, and it's a beautiful fall day outside. I wish I could take you for a walk. The trees have turned late this year. Remember how we used to do the color tours up north along M22? I always had so much fun with you."

"You're a funny man, Mr. McAllister. I don't recall you having fun on those outings with me. You were always in a hurry to get back to the hotel, if memory serves me correctly." Liza chimed back quickly only to mentally smack herself for falling into an old banter with Ledge.

The smirk disappeared from Ledge's face, but he wasn't angry with her comment. He was looking at the bucket. "Does that need to be emptied? If so, please hand that to me, and don't even think about up-ending it on me." With his "serious father" eyes, he looked pointedly at his captive ex-wife.

"Geez, Ledge." She sighed, retrieved the bucket, and set it in front of him. "Look, do you mind if I use the *real* bathroom? I gotta go."

He seemed to think about it for a moment, his eyes never leaving hers. Finally, he said, "I'll empty this first and then be back to get you." Picking up the pee bucket, he grabbed the doorknob behind him and pulled it toward him, without turning his back on her. He walked backward out of the room, quickly locking the door.

***

With the bathroom one door down on the other side of the hall, Ledge eyed his route, looking for any opportunities that Liza might seize for an escape. He saw nothing to worry him. Now for the bathroom itself. Emptying the bucket into the toilet, he flushed and glanced around. He spotted his razor, picked it up, and put it in his pocket. He checked the medicine cabinet, and, not finding anything that she could use as a weapon, he closed the cabinet door. He didn't bother to check under the sink and the other closet since he had packed it full of items for her to use for her stay. Picking up the bucket, he quickly rinsed it out, using some mouthwash to disinfect it, and then placed it in the tub upside down to dry. *I guess that will do until I have time to get a few more supplies from the store.*

He headed back to her room and opened the door. "Let's go, Liza-bear."

***

He held her arm all the way to the bathroom. She thought he might stand there and watch her for a moment, but when she entered, he shut the door, apparently waiting in the hall. She said a silent prayer of thanks for that small gift, and took a seat on the toilet to do her business, all the while looking around. When she'd finished, she immediately opened the medicine cabinet—nothing that would be useful to her there. *Where the hell is his razor? No windows in here either. What is wrong with this house!*

Frustrated, she washed her hands and stared at herself in the mirror, looking and feeling filthy. She was still wearing her airport clothes. Black slacks and a violet sweater. Suddenly, feeling bold, she shouted through the door. "Hey, I'm feeling gross. I'm going to take a shower while I'm in here." She had to assume he was standing there, right outside the door, like a certified creep.

"Go ahead," he said. "I bought your favorites; they're in the cupboard. Do you need help with your shower?" He sounded like the old Ledge, but she knew better. The new Ledge was sharp and tricky and crazy. *Tiptoe, Liza. Tiptoe.*

"I can handle it." Keeping her thoughts to herself.

"Holler if you change your mind. I'll be right here when you get done."

"Gotcha. I'll be fine." Liza shook her head in disbelief. *Creep! Why is he being so kind? What's he up to? He's acting like he used to—before the Cantril and our world tipped off its axis. Tiptoe, Liza.*

Turning toward the wall behind the door, she opened the cupboard. Five shelves filled with clothes, undergarments, and shoes. Running shoes. *How appropriate, because I'm gonna need those.* She smiled and pulled out a pair of jeans, a sweatshirt, and of course, the running shoes. He had made good choices size-wise. Everything should fit comfortably. For a fleeting moment, she wondered how he knew for sure what her size was. Then again, she had only dropped a few sizes since their divorce, so she let the thought fly away.

She pulled the shower curtain back, removed the bucket from the tub, and flipped on the water. It occurred to her only then that she could lock the door—but when she inspected the knob, it was clear that it could not be locked. She turned quickly back to the cupboard and flipped through each shelf swiftly and came up empty for any weapon, then whipped around to the cupboard under the sink. Still nothing she could use. Sighing heavily, Liza stripped off her clothes and stepped into the heavenly fall of hot water.

"You doing okay in there, sugar-bear?"

His voice jolted her. She'd forgotten he was standing right outside the door. And his use of that particular pet name sent a shiver along her spine. He'd used that term often, but in a mocking, hateful way, when he'd been on the Cantril and rage had overtaken him.

"Everything's great. Almost done." *Tiptoe, Liza.*

She got the hell out of the tub, dried off, and dressed hurriedly. "There are toiletries for you under the sink. All the stuff you like." Chills ran her spine as if he was watching her every move. She quickly eyed everything in the room to see if he had a camera installed anywhere in the small bathroom. Coming up empty, she returned to the cabinet under the sink. When she looked there earlier, she hadn't noticed the items were for her. This time she saw a toothbrush, toothpaste, a hairbrush ... all her basic essentials, but no makeup. *Of course.* He hated when she put on the "war paint."

"I see it all now. Thank you."

She brushed her teeth and long hair, squeezing out the water one more time with the towel. She threw her damp hair back up in the hair tie she had around her wrist and turned to face the door. To face the predator. *Breathe, Liza.*

She opened the door, a smile plastered on her face. "All done."

"You look refreshed. Quite lovely." He winked at her as he grabbed her arm and led her back to her room.

She thought about asking him for an upgraded room, given his pleasant demeanor, but she held back. *Tiptoe, Liza.* This had become her mantra.

She sat on the couch, feeling a little more alive than she had felt a half-hour ago. As she settled, her right hand brushed her left wrist. Her breath caught. Liza casually pulled her sweatshirt sleeve over the watch and tugged at her sleeve in the same manner so as not to arouse attention. Liza had all but forgotten she'd bought the fancy waterproof watch for her cruise. A friend of hers had recommended it so she didn't have to carry her cell phone when she was on the trip. It could make calls without her phone. Liza suddenly was itching to be alone so she could test the signal and try to get a message out. Thankfully, he hadn't taken her watch—yet. She was silently smacking herself for not remembering this yesterday.

Then it hit her—Chrissie would know she was missing! She would be looking for her! A smile absently crossed her face, and Ledge said, "What's that smile for, Liza-bear?"

She almost cursed herself for being so transparent. She attempted to divert her true thoughts into something that praised him. Best tactic, always.

"Oh, I was thinking about the time we stayed in that cabin our first year. You had picked quite the quaint getaway."

Ledge's eyes lit up and chuckled at that old memory. "Ah, yes … well, you didn't need all the clothes you had brought with you. You were thoroughly overdressed and over-packed that weekend."

This is feeling way too real, way too cozy. Liza's smiled faded. Things were reverting to the old days, and it was way too easy to fall back to feeling comfortable and safe. *Ledge is not safe. He's not to be trusted. Tiptoe, Liza You don't know what the hell is going on. And obviously that memory led to a dead end.* If they were near that cabin, his facial expression was not telling.

Ledge clapped his hands together and changed the subject, for which Liza was grateful. He said, "Now, how about breakfast? You still love Eggs Benedict?"

"Yes, I do. That would be great."

"Great, I'll go get it started." Ledge's face resembled that of the Cheshire cat up to no good.

"Would you like some help? I know how you don't like to cook."

"No, I've learned a lot. I just might surprise you, Liza-bear."

Smiling, he cautiously reached down and grabbed her food tray from the night before. He locked the door, leaving her sitting on the couch and trying to sort out her feelings about the situation she was in, the too-cozy conversation they'd been having, the old Ledge, the new Ledge. Coming up with nothing that could fully ease her mind, she instead focused on her escape. She withdrew the nail from between the cushions, but thought better of it, and quickly replaced it. Fidgeting, she finally walked to the door and listened for the sounds of him rattling around in the kitchen. But she heard nothing, which made her assume the kitchen was too far away for her to hear anything.

Remembering her watch, she quickly pulled her sleeve back and checked for a signal. Liza wandered around the tiny room, maneuvering her wrist high and low to no avail. It didn't look good for the home team. The area might be far enough removed from a cell tower, or this tomb of a room she was in was blocking a signal. She quickly put together a text to Trinity. She was the quickest path to her rescue. If she tried to place a call right now, Ledge might be right outside the door or walk in before she could get the call out. And worse, if she did reach 911 and hung up, they would call right back. Liza shuddered at the terrifying thought of how that would push Ledge over the edge. She didn't want to see the Demon.

No. No, that was on hold until she knew he was in a place that he wouldn't be checking on her or he was asleep. She quickly put that text out to Trinity and prayed as she watched the watch screen. The dreaded FAILED sign showed up on the screen. *Damn.* It'd have to wait. She had no clue as to where she was. Maybe up north somewhere? He had mentioned the autumn leaves. Was this a place he'd purchased to somehow please her? Maybe near that cabin they spent so much time in?

Liza paced like a caged panther, though there was not much room to do so. *Thank God, I'm not claustrophobic.* Thoughts were ebbing and flowing through her mind trying to figure out where she was. She finally stopped the pacing and started stretching, doing squats, feeling the burn. Preparing.

When the key sounded in the lock, she rushed back to the couch, keeping her breathing controlled.

"Breakfast is served," he said, entering with a tray of food.

***

Ledge balanced the tray carefully so he didn't spill the orange juice and closed the door. He had nixed the idea of hot coffee, just in case she decided to throw it at his face. Lizabeth slid over on the couch, making room for the tray. Smiling at her and to himself, he sat on the couch and placed the tray between them. He saw her eyes widen as he did so when she noticed there were two glasses of orange juice and two plates on the tray.

Liza slowly raised her eyes to look at him. *Is that a smile lurking there?* He could only hope. He dared to feel a smidgeon of victory. If he could show her how much he really loved her, maybe—just maybe—she'd take him back. Providing he could keep The Demon at bay, of course. That bastard had an uncanny way of showing up when he least expected it. Taking a deep breath, he let it out slowly and handed Lizabeth her silverware, which he'd rolled up in a napkin, exactly like the restaurants did.

"Thank you, Ledge. Breakfast looks really good."

Almost feeling giddy from her appreciative acknowledgment, he said, "You're very welcome." Not wanting to ruin the mood, he stopped there and let her eat. He did the same.

They ate in silence. It'd been so long since he'd had this kind of time with her, he didn't want to speak and break the spell. He was extremely happy to be here again with her. So many times, he'd tried to call her at work before the divorce was finalized, but she would have nothing to do with him. Her assistant and others in the office were keen to be vague and not give him information, always protecting her. Trinity wouldn't speak to him, and Oliver had lent him his ear but didn't offer to help him patch things up with her. According to Oliver, she was "done with him this time," that he had seen it in her eyes. Ledge had felt defeated, until today, this morning. *This beautiful morning.*

Lizabeth wiped at her mouth daintily and placed her napkin on the tray, her plate empty. Ledge had downed the last of the orange juice. She was staring at him with a look he didn't understand. "What's the matter, Liza-bear? Didn't you like it?"

"It was great. I'm surprised you did all this. The Eggs Benedict was perfectly prepared. Crispy bacon, too. All displayed like restaurant quality. It was very delicious."

"I'm so glad you enjoyed it. I've been working on my cooking skills lately." He bowed his head slightly, hopefully sending a gentle, charming impression. After all, he was gentle and charming. Except for when he wasn't. When he was the Demon. More than anything, though, he loved her with all his heart. He could not live without her; that had become increasingly clear to him since they'd been apart.

He stood and picked up the tray. "I'll take this and clean up the mess in the kitchen. Back soon."

She stood as well. "Do you need some help?"

He stopped in his tracks and pondered this offer—not quite sure if she was angling to get away or was truly trying to be helpful. She seemed genuine. *Why ruin what has started out to be a wonderful day?*

He looked her directly in the eyes before responding—seeing the beautiful face he'd fallen in love with and those honest eyes, "Yes, that would be nice."

A big smile covered her face, which lit his soul on fire.

"Great!" she said. "Let me carry the tray to the kitchen, and you can put me to work."

The good old days are here again. Could it be true? He suddenly felt dizzy— "swooning" like a Southern Belle—and was grateful when she took the tray.

In the kitchen, which he'd spent the last two months renovating in preparation for this day, he watched as she looked around. She was clearly impressed, speechless even.

She had always enjoyed cooking for him back in the day and constantly talked about updating their kitchen. Her schedule and his hadn't permitted that, but he was on his way to mending broken ties. He knew she was practically drooling as she looked at the new appliances and granite countertop. The only way to her heart was to show her by blessing her with something she had always wanted. All his hard work had to show her how much he loved her.

She finally turned to him with an awestruck expression, still holding the tray.

"Do you like it, Liza-bear?"

"Did you do all this?"

"Yes. All with you in mind." He took the tray from her and placed it on the countertop.

She followed, her hands gliding over the blue-flecked granite on the center island. "How did you know these are the colors I wanted to use? The whitewashed cabinets ... everything is exactly like I used to dream about."

Suddenly, she turned to him with a furrowed brow. "How did you know this? I mean, we talked about renovating, but I never told you *specifics*. How could you know?"

Smiling so big he could barely speak, he said, "I found your *Future Kitchen* folder in the drawer of the desk at home. You basically gave me the plans; I built it for you. Would you like the walk-through of all the fine details?"

Chapter 6

Astounded by all that bling in the kitchen, Liza let Ledge lead her around, showing her all the drawers and cabinets, and what they contained, one by one. The kitchen of her dreams was right there in front of her. Blinking back tears, she held herself together as she glanced inside the pantry cupboard, with its pull-out shelves accessible from both sides, and slide-out drawers. No more reaching in fumbling around for that lost pot lid.

The kitchen cabinets included slam-proof drawers, a skinny silverware drawer, and a utensil drawer ... everything she'd always wanted, right at her fingertips. The cobalt-blue fridge, a matching built-in microwave above the chef-size oven, a matching stovetop was set in the island next to a small second sink. It was all right there, no longer a dream. She knew this had cost a small fortune. She turned her large brown eyes to look at Ledge, "How did you manage this? I mean, with your work schedule and ... well, everything. The costs. I'm so ... shocked."

"Pleased?"

"Yes!" she said before she realized her response sounded like she was going to stay, would be cooking in this kitchen for a long time. The second she realized her small response created a promise, her stomach churned. She was treading water in an ocean of the unknown with no land in sight.

"I had some vacation days coming, so I used a week to get rid of the old and then weekends and nights to begin the build-out. After I got into a rhythm, it really went pretty quickly. I had a helper, too."

The wheels were turning in Liza's head. Why would he do this now? Why, after so long, did he finally make the time to give her something she had wanted so badly? To make her dream come true? Worse of all, why did she feel guilty for wanting to stick to her plan of escape? She was losing her grip on reality. Cue the Twilight Zone music.

Tiptoe, Liza. Tiptoe. This is not the old Ledge. Feeling uneasy and a little shaky, Liza sat down at the bar, which was built into the island. Placing her hand on the cool granite, she looked around at her beautiful dream.

Why did he build it here? Where was here? Tearing her eyes away from the details of the kitchen, she looked up at Ledge to see that primo smile still plastered to his face. That clothes-melting face, when he turned on the charm. Ledge. *Oh, how I wish you were really back.* She winced ever so slightly, hoping for things that couldn't be.

Ledge apparently caught the brief change in her demeanor, because he moved closer and placed his hand over hers. She warred between allowing it or pulling away. Before she could decide, he asked, "What's wrong, Liza-bear? Did I forget something?"

Hearing his pet name for her—stated with kindness and love—and with all this surrounding her, hearing the concern in his voice, and then remembering that she was essentially a prisoner here, she finally lost it. Tears streamed down her face, her shoulders shook, and a small sob escaped her lips. Liza put her hands to her face too late to conceal her distress.

Ledge quickly wrapped his arms around her and held her tight. "There, there, don't you cry. I don't want you to cry. I want you to be happy about this."

She remained stiff in his arms, not giving in, though she wanted to melt into them. She was tired. She was confused. Shaking harder, the tears continued. "Liza-bear, please don't cry. I thought this would make you happy? Are you happy? What can I do?"

She tried to contain herself enough to speak. The concern in his voice made it hard. She hadn't seen this side of him in such a long time. Gathering her strength to speak and not have her voice crack, she pulled away from him. "Ledge, you did make me happy. I am ... happy. With this." She wanted to add that she was unhappy with the situation. She wanted to ask him questions. But she feared what he may do if it tripped his switch.

And that was precisely why she must *tiptoe, Liza. Tiptoe.*

Wiping her tears from her face, Ledge leaned back and gazed at her for a long moment, before walking over to the built-in desk and pulling some tissues out of a drawer.

Handing them to her, she blew her nose and wiped her tears. Feeling balanced again, she whispered, "Thanks."

Ledge leaned in for a hug that she wasn't expecting. She allowed herself this little bit of peace, only for a second, because the Demon lurked somewhere nearby.

This is a rare moment. Don't get too comfortable.

***

Happy to have her in his arms again, Ledge was on a high he hadn't felt since his winning touchdown at the homecoming game during his senior year. He'd made the winning score that night with only a few seconds left on the clock.

She shifted slightly, and he reluctantly let her go. She looked up at him with those doe eyes he so loved, and he was almost ready to kiss her, when she moved to get off the chair.

"I guess I'd better get busy cleaning the kitchen like I promised."

"We'll do it together."

And they did. Like a normal, happy couple.

This needs to last. I need to keep this going. She's mine; she will always be mine.

Feeling bold, he snapped Liza playfully with a dish towel as she finished sponging down the counter next to the sink.

She reared around with fright in her eyes that quickly went away when she saw the teasing smirk on Ledge's face. "So that's how you're going to play this?" Laughing, she threw the sponge in the sink and swiped the other dish towel off the counter, twirling it, getting ready to snap him on the leg. He quickly moved in before she made her mark, grabbed her, and threw her over his shoulder—like he used to do when they were first married.

Howling with laughter, Liza cried, "Put me down, Mr. McAllister! Put me down now!"

Ledge ran around the kitchen with her. "As you wish, Mrs. McAllister." He pretended to spike her onto the kitchen floor. Liza's eyes were lit with playfulness as they both laughed at their favorite movie line from *Princess Bride*.

***

Liza had taken care to keep herself focused on her goal. She had recovered quickly after she'd fallen apart in Ledge's arms. That had been way too cozy, and she had pulled away in the nick of time. Yes, they'd had some fun a few minutes ago, goofing around, but she knew to keep her focus. To help her with that, she brought up the image of him bent over that ... slut.

She was folding the dish towels as he put away some dishes, when she remembered to get her bearings. Now was the time. She noticed that the windows in the kitchen—yes, by God, this room had windows—allowed the morning light to filter through. There was nothing but trees and other foliage from her view near the sink, so she still couldn't figure out exactly where she might be. But this at least told her that the right side of the kitchen faced eastward. That meant, when they walked into the kitchen from the hall, they were facing north.

She also noticed a door on the left side of the kitchen. It was an inside door, but she was unsure if it led to another room or maybe a mudroom, which would hopefully lead to the outside. On the south wall near the west-side wall was a swinging door that her logic dictated led to the dining room. The only other exit was back the way they had come—they had passed the living room on her right when they came through the hall. There were closed double doors on her left, opposite the living room. She assumed they opened to the dining room. Her mind was awash with all the house plans she had drawn in drafting class to help her visualize this house as a floor plan.

She was hoping to schmooze Ledge into getting a tour of the house. If so, she would inspect everything she could without being obvious. She was anxious to see if there were any other ways out. Possibly get a glimpse of the outside from other windows. The majority of the house felt like a cavernous tomb.

She prayed she could determine some possibilities for escape routes, but then came the next question: could she really make a run for it and succeed? Her short legs were no match for his. Besides, he was quick. He had been a wide receiver in high school and had always kept in shape.

She'd have to outsmart him if she was going to outrun him. Flirting might get her that opportunity. Two could play at the charm game, and as long as Happy Ledge was there, the Demon would hopefully stay away.

Chapter 7

Ledge was so tickled they were getting along. He wanted to pick her up and swing her around like he used to in high school, but he had already taken a chance by picking her up in the kitchen, and he didn't want to push his luck.

He couldn't wipe the smile off his face. Liza was turned away from him, hanging the towels on the pull-out towel rack under the counter next to the sink. He had seen that feature in her kitchen plans. Very efficient. He looked to the clock on the wall above the mudroom door and saw it was almost eleven. Astonished at how time had already flown, he was hoping they could go for a walk ... if she proved worthy.

Liza turned to him and smiled coyly. "So, what's the plan for today? Do you feel like giving me a tour of the place?"

He considered her query for a moment before answering. Sizing her up, he found her looking a lot more like her old self.

"I think that's a great idea. I have some more plans for this place, by the way. I'd love to get your opinion."

"And I'd love to give you one." She grinned playfully. "You know how I've always wanted to renovate an old home like this. How old is this house, anyway?"

"This is about sixty years old. Gramps built it for Gram. I was their only grandchild, so Gram left it to me when she passed away."

"I had noticed the furnishings and decor were older. So, what were you thinking of doing?"

"Well, the kitchen you've seen, so let's go check out the dining room. Gram didn't have a large family, but it'll fit ten people at the table comfortably. She wanted lots of grandbabies." He felt himself grow cold and shadowy for a moment, and he wondered if the Demon was creeping up on him. But no, no ... he had everything he had hoped for so far.

Everything was going according to plan, if not better. There would be no demon today.

Exiting the kitchen, they walked the short distance to the sliding double doors, which recessed into the walls. Liza peered into the dusty room as Ledge stood aside for her. "Go on in. There's dust everywhere. I didn't think there was any sense in cleaning since I'll be renovating it."

"I really like the double wooden doors. They add to the elegance of the woodwork on all the intricate tall baseboards and crown molding in this room. It would be nice to add frosted windows to them."

Ledge smiled. "I like that idea." Liza glanced at the old dining room table that was covered with a dust cloth. Seeing a swinging door in the corner of the room, she realized that her earlier thought had been accurate. That door led to the kitchen. There was a dark-walnut hutch filled with china and crystal, and she imagined more of the same below in the cabinets. There was also an old-style buffet table that matched the hutch.

The worn yellow-and-white-striped wallpaper was peeling in quite a few spots. It was like stepping back in time. Liza's eyes landed on the wall of dingy white curtains across the long table. She couldn't see outside. She wanted to pull them back to see if that was another door or bank of windows, but she caught Ledge eyeing her. He shifted himself to act like a tour guide, arm outstretched. "Shall I show you the living room?"

Liza stepped back out into the hall and followed Ledge a few steps through the pony walls that held up custom-built open shelving units. They acted as a grand entrance to the living room. The delicate spindles reached the ceiling on both sides of the entry to the spacious room.

She ran her hand along the shelving, not quite touching. "Did your Grandpa carve these? I remember you saying he had been a carpenter, right?"

"Yes, he carved those. Gram wanted something that would showcase his talent, so he put those in for her. She loved to show off how well he worked with wood. All the furniture in the dining room he made as well. When you're ready, we can work on that room. I don't feel like making a mess right now."

"I agree; that's a lot of dust in there." Smiling sweetly at him, she turned and walked further into the room and noticed that the gloomy curtains covered a large picture window on the east wall. The walls were covered in the oak paneling that was popular back then, making the room feel dark and foreboding. A shiver swept across Liza. Shaking it off, she moved toward the front door, acting as if she was looking at the framed family photos on the wall. There was one of Ledge with his parents and older brother. She suddenly felt Ledge behind her, and she startled. She hadn't heard him approach her. Chuckling, he put his hands on her shoulders as Liza turned toward the front door.

"This door ... it's beautiful," she said, trying to act comfortable, normal. "I'm going to assume he did this as well?"

"Yes, he did." Taking her right hand, he gently set it flat on the door so she could feel the wood and the carvings his grandfather had done. Liza breathed slowly, trying hard not to recoil from his touch. She quickly noted there was a dead bolt in addition to the fancy but tarnished doorknob.

"Such intricate woodwork. Did you learn anything from him?"

"Sadly, no. He passed away before I was old enough to get to know him. I barely remember him. I was six, maybe. All his tools are still in the outbuilding in the shop, which he'd made for himself. Maybe someday I'll learn how to use them."

As Ledge turned her toward the hallway, Liza thought about the tools that could be in that shop as her eyes washed over the rest of the living room. The ghostly furniture covered in dusty sheets, a large shag rug in the center of the room, an old box TV set, oak end tables, and what appeared to be an old record player were also in attendance.

He said, "Come. I'll show you the bedrooms."

A handful of steps past the living room wall, Ledge stopped at the first door on the same side as the living room. Which was directly across from the bathroom door. "This is my room. I always stayed here in the summer for a week or when mom and dad went away for a trip. Gram used to have a bunk bed for John and me in here. But she had someone bring this bed in after John died. And it wasn't too long after that when she came to live with me. I haven't been back here until now."

Liza glanced around the room while Ledge spoke her mind whirring from all the facts she was accumulating. His voice had grown small as he talked about his brother. She knew he missed him. She saw the pain in his eyes when he stopped talking. He turned toward the door, and then, as if realizing where he was and what he was doing, he turned back to Liza and took her hand. Under the circumstances, a small gesture was all she could muster. She squeezed his hand and released her grip, but he held on. Age-old habits die hard, and Liza wasn't about to break the trance Ledge was under. Hand-holding used to be their *thing*.

She looked around the room and noticed a door in the far corner. *Must be a closet*. Ledge turned them toward the bedroom door.

"Down here is Gram's room, the master suite sans a bathroom. She didn't feel comfortable adding one when it was only her and Gramps living here. Plus, she wouldn't have been able to have her walk-in closet."

Liza noticed this room was across from the door she had exited that morning. Walking into the master bedroom was like stepping back in time to her grandma's room. The walls were painted in pale pink, with a few pictures on the walls. The dresser was old-fashioned, possibly a family heirloom. Her grandma had owned one in a similar style: the dark-stained bureau with a towel rack and a blue-and-white washbasin on top. There was another older-style dresser with the same dark wood stain on the other side of the room. To their right was a walk-in closet. It extended the whole length of the wall.

She couldn't shake the feeling as she walked through the house that something was "off," particularly with the bedrooms. *I can't put my finger on it*. Before she could put more thought into the floorplan, Ledge interrupted her.

"Grams loved the walk-in closet. She had a thing for clothes and hats." He opened the right side of the closet to show the many cubby-style shelves filled with old hat boxes. Picking one up from the top shelf, Ledge pulled the box down to Liza's level. "Go ahead; open it."

Liza reached for the top of the hatbox that was covered in a light film of dust. She daintily set the lid down on an open shelf and gingerly picked up the hat. She marveled at the pheasant feathers that plumed from one side and turned it in her hands to take in the beauty and work that went into such a creation. "It's beautiful."

"Try it on."

Liza shook her head. "I couldn't."

"It's okay. Gram wouldn't mind."

Gently lifting it, she hesitated a few seconds before letting it settle on her head. Ledge set the hatbox down on the shelf with the box lid and walked her over to the mirror that was behind the door. She gasped at how pretty the hat looked on her.

"Gram would be smiling from ear to ear right now, seeing how well you wear that hat. It was one of her favorites. One of many." Ledge chuckled. "Gram used to wish we boys were girls so she could dress us up in her girlie wear, like these hats. But Gramps liked his hats, too, so she settled for us dressing up in his hats and things."

Turning from the mirror, Liza removed the hat and walked back to the box to gently set it back in its place. She handed the box back to Ledge after securing the lid. He put it back in its rightful place. She saw pain on his face, and he didn't erase it after he brought his eyes back to Liza's. *Oh, Ledge, I wish I could comfort you, but this is not right. Not now.*

She lowered her gaze and moved to leave the closet. Ledge stopped her by wrapping his strong arms around her, practically forcing a hug from her. She acquiesced and hugged him back. The storm was brewing; she could feel it buzzing from within him. *Tiptoe, Liza.* Hair raised on the back of her neck as she stood stock-still, waiting for him to release her.

After what felt like forever, Ledge finally stepped away, his smile bright and friendly as he gazed down at her. Feeling uncomfortable, she smiled back and started to exit the closet. This time, he let her pass and followed her, but not without grasping her hand as they left Gram's room.

***

Ledge smiled at Lizabeth as he led her down the hall and back toward the kitchen. He hadn't shown her the mudroom yet. That held the door to the back porch. She had been calm and understanding of his needs so far. She was so beautiful in Gram's hat that he really wanted to take her back to his room and ravish her. Sadly, he knew he had more work to do before that could happen. She kept looking at him with doubt in her eyes, yet she never asked any questions.

She will see the changes soon, and we'll be together again, forever.

Chapter 8

Sitting at the kitchen island, Liza peered out the window while Ledge made a very late lunch. It was four in the afternoon, and Ledge was calm—too calm. She felt uneasy watching him whisk around the kitchen. *I have no idea how he learned to cook and so well, but it has certainly paid off.* She inhaled the scents of the meal he was preparing. He had sliced the veggies like a professional chef. The simmering blue pot of homemade red sauce smelled intoxicating, and the pasta shells were stuffed with a rich ricotta mixture. He barely looked at Liza as he pulled the plates to start serving the food. She didn't want to break the spell he seemed to be under while he worked, so she sat and watched, not making a peep.

Finally, Ledge had everything ready and grinned like a kid in a candy store as he handed her the perfect plate of pasta. She thanked him as he came around the island and sat next to her. Taking her hand, he prayed, "Thank you, Lord, for this food and for Lizabeth. I pray you keep the kids safe. Amen." He released her hand and grinned. "Dig in, Liza-bear."

"It looks so delicious. I'm definitely digging in." And she did, groaning with pleasure at the first bite. She didn't care that her tongue was slightly burnt from the hot sauce.

Ledge laughed. "You see? I've learned a lot over the past few months, haven't I?"

She nodded, her mouth full.

"I can't wait to make you more meals or help you make your famous lasagna."

She swallowed, took a sip of water, and then said, "It's very clear you've learned a whole bunch. These are the best stuffed shells I've ever tasted."

"I'm so glad you like it."

Not much more was said as they both dug in and ate like it was their last meal. Liza had set her fork down, stuffed to the brim, when Ledge said, "Dammit! I forgot the garlic bread. Dammit." He threw his fork down on the counter, and Liza sat back to ease away from Ledge, away from the threat of the onset of anger.

"Ledge, I'm so full, even if you *had* made the garlic bread, I wouldn't have been able to eat it. The meal was wonderful without it."

"But I had the bread all made and ready in the freezer. It's perfect!"

Thinking quickly, Liza smiled sweetly at him and said, "I'm sure it is perfect. If we make my famous lasagna tomorrow, it'll go great with that. Yeah?"

Thankfully, Ledge's eruption was small and limited. He seemed to calm after a moment, and he turned to her, smiling. "Yes, it will go great with your lasagna. We can definitely make that tomorrow for lunch. I promise I won't bother you while you cook it. I'll watch and learn."

The darkness she'd witnessed a minute ago was washed away, just like that. Breathing a sigh of relief, she stepped down from her perch at the island and started to clear the plates. Ledge followed suit, and they had the kitchen cleaned in no time.

She was about to ask, "So, what's next?" when Ledge grabbed her left hand and bent down on his right knee. The action so surprised her that she gasped, taking in a mouth full of air and saliva. She choked on it, coughing relentlessly until she was able to sip on some water.

Coughing jag over, Ledge was still on his knee, waiting patiently, smiling wide.

What the ...?

From behind his back, he pulled a shiny object that sparkled in the lights that hung over the kitchen sink. She quickly realized what it was and almost choked again at another quick intake of air. Somehow, she managed to maintain her composure. It was nothing short of a miracle that she was able to.

Ledge held up her wedding ring that she'd set on the counter the day she left him. "Liza-bear, I have worked hard the past few months, for this day. I've fixed everything I can fix. And the only thing left to fix is this. You and me. I can't wait any longer for you to wear my ring again."

She stared at the ring gleaming at her, almost leering at her. She had no words.

He continued. "Today has been such a blessing to me. The day you left, I felt empty inside. I vowed I would find a way to win you back. I need you in my life. I can't live without you. Please." Ledge got quiet when he ended with, "Please, will you wear my ring?"

Liza had heard every word, every beautiful word—and she found the sentiment to be lacking. Lacking remorse. An apology. Not one "I'm sorry" in there for him screwing everything that walked, for the way he'd treated her. He hadn't asked for her hand in marriage; he'd asked her to put the ring back on, as if the divorce had never happened.

Their eyes were connected. She could not bring herself to shift her gaze, so intrigued was she with the display in front of her. This man, his words. The weirdness of it all. In a million years, this "proposal," or whatever it was, would have been the last thing she could imagine happening to her. Especially after he'd drugged her, kidnapped her, brought her here, and locked her in a room. Liza's skin began to crawl.

Ledge's face was unreadable. She knew what she had to do. She nodded, not able to bring herself to speak. If she opened her mouth, she knew a scream would come out, rather than warm words.

Ledge's expression told her he was pleased, a wide grin splitting his face as he slid the ring on her finger. She'd not seen that face since the day he'd *really* proposed so many years ago. "Liza-bear! You've made me the happiest man in the world!" he hollered as he jumped up and grabbed her around the waist, threw her over his shoulder, and started his victory dance around the island.

She'd almost hurled up her food before he finally set her down—after three laps around the kitchen. But she kept her game face on and smiled. She knew if she rocked the boat, things would turn ugly quicker than a hummingbird's wings zipped through the air.

Unease rested low in her gut, and a headache was starting to thrum at her temples. She wasn't sure if it was all the twirling, or if it was the fact that she was stuck in the middle of nowhere with a man who scared the living shit out of her. One wrong word could send him over the edge. One wrong move, one wrong *anything* was all it would take. The weight of the ring on her finger was as heavy as her heart.

She'd seen him battling his temper over a simple thing like garlic bread. She'd also seen him regain his facade, for her. It was all there. She saw the signs. She knew. She had begged him to seek help and to get off the medication after it became apparent what it was doing to him. Cantril had screwed him up—was still affecting him—and she was going to pay the price for that. She could feel it. A shiver ran down her spine.

I have to find a way out. A safe way out. God help me.

Tiptoe, Liza. The eggshells are covering the floor.

Chapter 9

Ledge had broken into a sweat from twirling her and running around the island. He wiped his brow and gazed upon his Lizabeth. His Liza-bear. His forever. He knew she couldn't resist him. Marriage was merely a piece of paper. Love was forever. She still loved him, and he could live with that, but he couldn't live without her. No one was going to take what was his. No one. Looking outside the kitchen window, he realized their walk was not going to happen today. It was already dark, and they'd missed the sunset, too.

"Tomorrow we'll take that walk in the woods; the trees are in full color. And I have a surprise for you on the back porch, but it'll keep until tomorrow. Tonight, we'll relax. I'll break out my old board games. Come and help me pick out a few games." He grabbed her left hand and felt the ring there, back where it belonged. His heart was melting as she smiled back at him. *Mine, all mine, forever.*

He led her down the hall to his room. He flicked on the light and headed toward the closet, where a stack of games was on the shelf. "We'll take two for now. I pick The Game of Life. What would you like?" Ledge turned to her, gleefully waiting for her decision. He couldn't wait to play.

She pointed at the Clue game and started to reach for it, but Ledge grabbed it, releasing her hand in the process. He then took down his game. Before he switched off the light, his eyes drifted to his bed, and he contemplated rekindling the fire with her tonight. Shaking his head, he glanced at Lizabeth and realized she hadn't spoken a word since he'd put the ring on her finger.

He frowned. In fact, she hadn't said "yes"—only nodded. He swallowed hard and tamped down the rising anger. He was not going to let his temper get the better of him tonight.

He flicked off the bedroom light.

They walked back through the house and into the kitchen, where he placed the games on the kitchen table. "Liza-bear, would you like a glass of wine? I have your favorite chilling in the fridge."

"That would be nice. Thank you."

Her voice seemed strange to him, stilted, emotionless. But perhaps he was reading too much into it. He was going to remain reasonable and positive. "Coming right up! Will you set up the Clue game?"

"Sure."

"I also have a cherry pie in the fridge for later, if you have a hankerin'."

"That sounds great. I haven't had pie in quite a while."

He filled the wineglasses and came back to the table. Lizabeth had the game all set up and was ready to play. "Here you are, Liza-bear."

"Thanks, Ledge."

"No problem. I see you're Miss Scarlet tonight. I think I'll be Colonel Mustard. You can go first."

"Sounds good."

Lizabeth rolled the dice and then took a sip of wine. Ledge breathed a sigh of relief. She was talking to him and smiling at him. There was nothing wrong. She was fine, happy even. All was finally right again in the world.

She is mine. All mine. Forever.

***

Taking another sip of her wine, Liza let it relax her. She prayed she didn't mess something up. She wasn't going to get drunk tonight—that was for certain—but a glass or two would help ease the tension that had built up in her head. Her temples were still throbbing, but at least she could breathe again. It was hard to play the "Happy Wife" act. She was going to have to be on her best behavior. She had caught Ledge glancing at her curiously several times. She'd worried that she'd blown it, but he seemed okay now—though, definitely possessive.

Her mind reflected on the choices of board games in the closet. It was a minefield of games that, if he failed to win, would surely bring forth the Demon. She about choked when he said he wanted to play the Life game. She was thankful it wasn't Battleship, Mouse Trap, Connect Four, Trouble, or even worse, Operation. A tremor ran through her at the thought of the last game. Liza mentally wiped her brow, hoping she'd dodged a bullet with her choice.

She had forgotten how strong he could be. He was always in control and quite the competitor. He didn't like to lose. It didn't matter what he was doing, he had to be the leader. He was great at a lot of things, and it didn't hurt that he could charm the pants off anyone. The success of his advertising agency, McAllister Designs, was proof of his charm and savvy.

Thinking back, she had liked that quality in him—the "leader" quality. Now, it was not high on her list. Back in the day, Ledge had balanced it with caring for others, too. It wasn't always about being in charge. Somewhere along the line, that had changed. Maybe it was his way of managing the pain of losing his family; he needed to control his surroundings. Maybe the fact that she wasn't able to have any more kids after the twins were born. That had deeply upset them both. Then the Cantril came about, so he could quit smoking. That medicine had created the anger-fueled creature from hell that she'd never seen in him before.

At least, that was her take on things. Sure, he had always been quick to anger, but it was infrequent and only when he was overwhelmed—just like any other person out there. But the Cantril seemed to multiply that anger a hundred times over. And when the switch was flipped, there was no stopping him. He couldn't remember what he'd done, and there was never an apology. He would act like nothing had happened. Even when Liza carefully replayed his actions to him, he could only remember bits and pieces. And, still, no apology.

This, tonight, was something out of a horror film. It was as if she were watching the scenes unfold from a movie-theater seat. She saw the pain on his face, the wariness in him, waiting to see what her response would be to this or that. The tension in his jaw and veins popping out in his neck while he waited to hear her say something. Would it be what he wanted to hear? Or not?

She was scared overall, but even more petrified that Ledge would try to take her to bed. She had seen him eye his bed for a brief moment—could almost read his thoughts. She held back another shudder that wanted to creep through her body.

Hearing the dice drop on the board, she focused back on the game and realized she was chewing on her fingernail. Pulling her nail out of her mouth, she sat on her hand while Ledge moved his yellow pawn. She reached with her free hand for the glass of wine, emptying it and placing it back on the table.

"Are you ready for a refill?" he asked.

"I can get it. You sit. Are you ready for pie?" Liza needed to do something besides sitting there, fretting, pretending to enjoy this stupid game.

"I'll help. I can get the plates if you pull the pie and wine."

Grabbing the glasses, he got up from the table and placed them on the island. She pulled the dessert and wine out of the fridge and refilled their glasses, while Ledge cut the cherry pie, complete with a fancy design cut into the top crust. It sure looked tasty. She placed the cork back on the bottle and put it back in the fridge. Ledge handed her a plate of pie before she'd even closed the door.

"This looks delicious, Ledge."

"I hope you like it. I know how much you love cherry pie."

With the two of them settled back at the table, she lifted her fork and took a bite.

"Delicious."

"I agree."

And back to the game they went. The happy couple. Miss Scarlett and Colonel Mustard.

Chapter 10

Ledge put the board games away. It was nearly 1:30 in the morning when they'd finished playing. He felt like a champion. He had won his Liza-bear back, and he had won at both Clue and The Game of Life. Liza had played well, though. He had lucked out, and his car was overfilled with kids when he pulled into the mansion on the last game. His mind wandered to the day he and Lizabeth had heard the depressing news. They were not going to be able to conceive again. She had to have a hysterectomy. It had crushed their future plans for having a house full of children. Ledge didn't want to adopt. He couldn't bear the thought of being denied by an adoption agency.

He had seen too many colleagues leaving the country to make their dreams come true after being told "no" here in the States. He had never told Lizabeth that little secret. His fears had selfishly held them back from filling their home with more little feet running around. He hated that he had done that to her. He shook his head and brushed his hands down his face, trying to replace the sadness in his heart with a fake smile.

Ledge now stood in the hall wearing his pajama bottoms, waiting for Lizabeth to come out of the bathroom. He had decided during The Game of Life that he wouldn't try to bed her tonight. He sensed she was a little on edge and wanted her to feel safe. He also figured that tomorrow, after the fresh air, the walk down the path of colorful trees, and the beautiful sunset on the back porch, she'd be putty in his masterful hands.

He was looking forward to tomorrow. Today had been an accomplishment of great proportions. Tomorrow, he would seal the deal. A real smile appeared on his face.

Liza emerged from the bathroom in a cotton PJ top—one of his own. He wanted to remind her how she had loved to wear his shirts to bed when she was pregnant with the twins. He had been bummed she wouldn't walk around naked, with her beautiful, swelled body carrying the seeds he had planted. He loved every inch of her, no matter how pregnant she was, but she'd insisted that she felt like an elephant on stork legs. Gazing at her now in the oversized shirt, she looked as beautiful as the day he first set eyes on her.

"Looks like it fits." Smirking at her.

"Very funny. I see what you did here, and thank you for that." Liza doe-eyed him and turned the corner of her lips up in half a smile.

"Come, let's call it a night." He took her hands and walked backward into his room, watching the expressions play across her face.

"Ledge, I …"

"Nope, we've both had a long day, and I know that couch couldn't have been comfortable last night, so you're sleeping with me. My bed isn't so bad, and I promise I'll let you sleep. Scouts honor." He raised two fingers and saluted.

"You're no Boy Scout, Ledge." She chuckled.

He quirked an eyebrow. "True."

He led her to the opposite side of the bed, closest to the closet. He wanted to be the one between her and the door. That was his place, to protect her. He pulled the covers back and tucked her in, snatching a quick kiss from her soft lips. He almost went back for more but saw her startled look.

"Sorry, I've never been able to resist your lips." Grinning, he made his way around to his side. He had decided not to make his usual move, which was to jump on the bed and crawl slowly over her to his side. He felt her eyes on him as he walked around the bed and slid beneath the covers. He turned to look her in the eyes. "Goodnight, sleep tight, don't let the bed bugs bite."

"Got it." She was smiling, a tiny bit.

She must be so tired.

Ledge reached for the lamp on his nightstand and cut off the light. He heard Liza yawn, as she rolled over on her side, facing the closet. He rolled over, too, but faced the door. He was too wired to sleep, even though the alarm clock lightly glowed a red 2:30 a.m.

Today was a gamble that had turned into a big win. He willed himself to relax as he thought about the coming day. A salacious smile bloomed on his lips.

Chapter 11

Liza lay awake, listening for Ledge to fall asleep. She was tired, but fear kept her eyes open. She'd used a fake yawn to punctuate to Ledge that she was tired. She had slowed her breathing, mimicking a deep slumber. When he'd rolled over, her heart filled with relief. He wasn't going to press her for more. It was almost too good to be true.

She waited and waited and waited ... until she was certain he was asleep. Her clothes were at the ready in the bathroom, and a flashlight was waiting for her in the kitchen drawer next to the sink. She had happened upon it while trying to put away the morning's dishes. She envisioned herself slipping out of the room, into her clothes, and through the door in the kitchen—which she prayed led to the outside. It had to. This was her escape plan, because to use the front door next to Ledge's room would wake him up if that door was swollen and hard to open from lack of use.

Please, God, let this work.

Ledge snorted, startling Liza. She lay as still as a rug, holding her breath. He rolled onto his back, and his breathing resumed to lightly snoring. She let the air out of her lungs slowly. Breathing steadily, she regained her calm. *It won't be long now.* Lying there another half hour or so, Liza tested the waters. She rolled on to her back. Ledge still snored. So Liza moved again, back to her side, facing the closet, and made sure to jiggle the bed a bit as she did so. Ledge snored away and never even shifted. He was in the zone. Once he was there, she could move around lightly, and he wouldn't notice. Unfortunately, he never slept for long. Time was ticking.

Liza pulled the covers back and slipped out of bed. The box springs squeaked a little when she reached the edge of the bed. She stopped and waited. There was nothing but snoring coming from his side of the bed. She smoothed the covers back and tiptoed out of the room and into the darkness of the rest of the house. But she knew the layout. The bathroom was straight ahead. Away she went, putting the plan in action.

Flashlight in hand, she moved toward the door in the kitchen, tried the knob. It didn't make a sound as it turned. She was going into this blind; she didn't know what was beyond this door—not for sure. It was a guess; this door had a draft sweep at the bottom, so she assumed it led to the outside.

Liza didn't open the door far. She inched her way through the opening and was able to step completely inside without running into anything. Quietly closing the door, she clicked the flashlight on and dulled it by covering it with her sweatshirt.

Her heart rammed in her chest as she looked around.

A mudroom of sorts. And a door that led to the outside.

Reaching for the door handle, she found it locked. Panic started in her blood, and then she realized the knob had the lock on her side. She unlocked it and turned the knob again. Relief washed through her when the cold fresh air hit her.

Freedom. Freedom!

The steps off the deck were right in front of her. She fanned the flashlight to her left and right, examining the layout of the land and listening for critters. There was nothing in sight except woods as far as she could see. No movement in the overgrown yard.

She took a moment to address the doorknob, turning the lock and pulling the door shut; hopefully, this would slow Ledge down a tad when he awoke and found her gone.

She didn't want to think about that for too long—how angry he'd be. She kept moving. Once on the east side of the house, she fanned the light around and saw a barn, but no vehicle. The lawn was a mass of overgrowth, and there was barely any visible gravel for a driveway. There were tracks ... well, more like mashed grass, and this had to be from a vehicle. She wished she knew where the damn car was. The barn? Maybe. But as she thought about it some more, that would be more noise and trouble than she was willing to risk. There had to be a house around here where she could get the help she needed.

Remembering her watch, Liza flashed the light on it to see if she had any bars to try to make a call once she figured out where she was. Still nothing, and the battery level was down to thirty percent. Swearing to herself, she sprinted into the woods and prayed they led her to safety.

Chapter 12

Monday

Ledge woke with a start. Feeling the bed beside him, it was cold, empty. Melancholy took hold of him for a moment before he bolted upright and into action. He tore off the sheets and leaped from the bed, flipped on the bedside lamp. He scanned the room. No Liza.

Not in the hallway. Not in the bathroom. Not in the kitchen.

Not in the house.

The reality was like a hard slap to his face, which had turned red with rage.

Furious with himself for trusting her, he stalked back into the bathroom. He found the PJ top on the floor. He picked it up and tore it in two, three parts. His blood boiled.

The Demon had returned.

Snorting like a bull, he ran to the front door. It was still locked, dead bolt and all. He scrambled for the back door, slipping on the floor in the hall as he turned toward the kitchen. "Damn it!" He ran back to the bedroom, threw on his jeans from the night before, and grabbed a white sweatshirt from the dresser drawer.

He glanced at the clock on the nightstand—6:45 a.m. The sun would be rising soon, but the woods hid it well. He quickly jammed his feet into his Hickies laced running shoes and dashed to the kitchen to grab the flashlight from the drawer.

But the flashlight was gone. He entered the mudroom, found another flashlight, and then headed for the back door. When he pulled on the doorknob, his hand slipped off.

She locked the damn door behind her! The bitch! Huffing loudly, he unlocked the door and stalked through the opening, slamming the door behind him, its little window shaking from the impact.

He scanned the area, looking for telltale signs of her path. Tracking her like an animal. Sure enough, he saw it—the disturbed grass that had surely been caused by her.

Gram didn't have much in the back yard by way of ornaments, and there were no shrubs next to the wraparound porch. His path was clear to the front of the house. Once there, he saw she had tamped down more overgrowth. It appeared she was trying to figure out which way to go. He saw marks heading down the driveway. He jogged ahead and then lost the tracks. He growled out, "Lizabeth!" No answer, and he hadn't expected one. It felt virtuous to bark her name.

He retraced his steps. It would be a while before he'd see the sun overhead. Scanning the yard again, he focused on the grass, still wet with dew. *There!* He saw a small path leading toward the opening in the woods. *Gotcha, my little tiger!* Picking up his pace, he headed in that direction, keeping to her path. "Lizabeth! I'm right behind you! Come out, come out, wherever you are!"

He kept his eyes glued to the path and surrounding foliage. Signs of disturbance, footprints, anything. It seemed like she was keeping to the old trail Gramps had made for Gram. He knew it led back to the small creek that bordered the property. If she stuck to the trail, he'd reach the creek as the sun was coming up. Maybe sooner. It'd been years since he'd gone down this path with Gram—he was only a child at the time, but he remembered it fairly well. He was quicker now, stronger, and that would be to his advantage, of course. If she'd taken the driveway, he could have lost her when she hit the main road.

Bad choice, Liza-bear.

Snapping twigs under his feet, he slowed his pace as he reached a large tree blocking the path. He ran the flashlight down the rotted tree trunk, looking to see where Lizabeth had made a move to climb over the tree. The tree roots dangled in the air, and there were small footprints in the earth near the roots. He followed those around the uprooted tree, back toward the path. As he picked up the pace again, he saw something else on the trail straight ahead.

He reached the spot that had caught his attention. A freshly dead animal lay on the path—a rabbit. He then noticed blood around the scene. Fanning the flashlight around him, he glared into the woods—was there anything watching him, ready to pounce? He listened but heard only the natural quiet of the woods.

He left the bunny kill to whatever had attacked it and kept on the path. Most times, it was a coyote out there. Wolves were not known to be in Lower Michigan. But bears were, and they were in an area where sightings occurred infrequently. Cougars were also known to show up unannounced from time to time. He prayed it was a coyote who'd been the hunter. The thought of Lizabeth being mauled hastened his pace. What had she been thinking, going into the woods in the dark? It worried and angered him at the same time. He kept thinking of the bunny.

And he kept hunting for his woman. He ran smoothly and at a good pace now, the trail unfettered. Finally, he saw the tree that yawned over the trail, under which Gramps had built a bench for Gram to rest upon before reaching the creek. It was a nice place because the woods opened up a little. She would leave yarn and other fluffy items here for the birds to gather for their nests. These were fond memories for Ledge; any memory of Grams was, in fact, a fond one. She had always taken time to teach him about nature—and the bears and coyotes.

Ledge traveled on down the path. Light was starting to break. Soon, the flashlight would not be necessary. The trail narrowed, and he finally arrived at where the woods opened up, and the creek was before him, barely moving, a ripple here and there. He took a minute to peruse the general area, see if he could tell where Lizabeth had gone from here. Seeing brush and weeds knocked down to his right, he started eastward along the creek. He proceeded with a bit more caution now—the creek's bank was filled with rocks and holes, and the pucker brush was thick. He raised his arm to shine the flashlight beam high and around him. Her tracks followed the creek.

Tracing her steps, he finally made it past the thorny brush, and the path alongside the creek became grassier and easier to navigate. He glanced up and ahead of him, and to his delight, he saw a light bouncing around out there.

Gotcha.

He turned off his flashlight to focus on the light he had seen farther down the creek. There it was again. He picked up his pace. He was halfway there when he called out, "Lizabeth! I see you!" He couldn't resist.

The light went dark. Standing on the side of the creek, he could barely make out a small figure in the dawn of the day. He stood stock-still, listening. She was maybe two hundred yards away from him now, moving into the woods.

Ledge smirked and quickly followed.

Chapter 13

Run! Run! Run!

She was panicked, desperate, losing hope. He'd seen her. He was right on her. She could hear his breathing. She tripped over a limb and felt the sting of twigs and dirt in her palms. She pushed herself up, fear and anxiety pulsating through her veins, her eyesight dimming with the tension. As she got to her knees, he hit her full-on, his torso covering her back. He used his weight to hold her down.

She lifted her head, could feel heat making its way down her cheek—blood. She wiggled, trying to escape, but there would be none of that. She finally decided to play possum, unmoving, "dead."

He tickled her.

He's freaking tickling me! What the hell?

There was no way she could not move. She shifted and jerked, and he kept on.

Another competition, and he's won again.

She began to weep as his maniacal laughter filled the silent morning air and echoed back through the trees.

The light went out inside her, and she suddenly felt nothing at all.

"Dead."

***

I feel energized. The run was what I needed to get my body humming and clear my head. Unfortunately, she will try to run again. I need to be on my toes next time. This does not change my plans. She will submit and be mine again. Or neither of us will survive.

***

These blackouts were taking their toll on Ledge. He didn't remember how he had happened to be carrying Lizabeth out of the woods and into the house. The last thing he remembered was realizing she had escaped.

After tucking her onto the couch in her room, he spent some time pacing in the kitchen, considering his options, thinking about what had happened, what he remembered, what he did not remember, what would happen now. He stopped at the fridge. Cooking had become his calm. Ledge began to focus on the numerous meals he had prepared this summer at the gourmet cooking class he had taken. His thoughts quieted as he pulled out everything he needed to prep the soup for supper. Cutting the veggies, he nicked his finger. Seeing the blood reminded him that Lizabeth had been bleeding.

He looked up, staring at the wall in front of him. *I must tend to her.*

***

Hearing the key in the lock, Liza groaned, knowing she had no energy left to fight. Her body was wrung out, her will and hope right along with it. No broken bones, she didn't think. Maybe some bruised ribs from when he'd landed on her. But her spirit—that was another story. Not moving an inch, she feigned sleep.

"I'm here to patch you up, sleeping beauty."

Yeah, yeah, yeah. There's no patching me up, buddy boy.

She continued her shallow breathing. Thought maybe, just maybe, she'd have another chance. Maybe. For now, she would let him do his thing.

Until she felt a searing pain on her forehead.

Her arms flew up and out, and she sat bolt upright.

"What the hell are you doing?" she screamed. She reached for her forehead and removed a small cloth. *Iodine. It's only iodine.*

Exhausted, she gave him one blank look, closed her eyes, and fell back on the couch.

She felt his cool hands clean up the gash on her head and wipe the dried blood from her face. He was a master at "making things right." The idea almost made her laugh out loud. All the years they'd been together, whenever he'd messed up, he would find a way to "make it right" with her. He could be a tender person when he wasn't in demon mode. Her mind drifted back to when they'd first met in high school. Rough football player that he was, he liked to dominate the field. He liked to dominate anything in his life. And he had. Including her.

And that need for control was alive and well in Gram's House of Hell.

***

Ledge gave her one long once-over before he stepped out of the room and locked the door behind him. She had always been his "beauty," sleeping or not. He'd fallen in love with her the moment he first saw her back in high school at the bonfire. It was love, wasn't it? What else could it be? He needed her back in his life, forever. She was his reason for living, breathing, and without her, he didn't want to go on. Touching the door handle quietly, he tested the lock. Reassured, he ignored the veggies he had started to cut for supper and grabbed his car keys. Locked the kitchen door behind him and ran to his car. It was less than twenty-five minutes to town, but he needed to get there and back before she woke. Driving down the old dirt road, he memorized his shopping list.

Dust flying, he came upon the main road in no time. Now he had to watch his speed. *Last thing I need is to be pulled over.* He glanced down quickly to check himself—was he fully dressed? Did he look like a maniac?—and that was when he saw he had some blood on his sweatshirt. Lizabeth's blood.

Reaching over the back of the seat, he prayed he had his jacket with him. Slamming on the brakes, he blasted his horn at the inconsiderate jerk who'd pulled out right in front of him. Muttering obscenities, he glanced back and saw the jacket lying on the floor.

Reaching the Handy Mart, he pulled into a parking spot far enough away from the outside cameras. He donned his ball cap and quickly slid his blue jacket over the sweatshirt. He zipped it up, effectively covering the blood. Looking in the rearview mirror, he checked his face. Everything was as it should be. He opened the car door and made haste toward the Handy Mart, keeping his head down.

Not only were there security cameras on the outside of the building, but there was one near the front door and one near the checkout counter on the inside as well. He had to be cautious. He was, after all, a kidnapper.

But, really, he was only bringing his beloved home to him. That wasn't kidnapping. Not really.

***

Liza woke up with a searing headache. She sat up slowly and reached for her temples to massage them. The cut on her forehead pounded, thwarting her efforts for relief. She gave up and glanced at her watch: 5:30 p.m. *Just another day in the dungeon.* To make matters worse, her battery power was nearing a critical level. Her one link to freedom was fading fast. She hadn't made it far enough to get a signal or find a house of refuge. Feeling sick to her stomach, she gave way to the tears. She didn't care if Ledge came in and saw her crying like a baby. She felt defeated. His words rang in her head:

"You're mine, Lizabeth! You don't get to leave me like you did!"

She remembered going to a bar once with him, back when they were dating, and he'd seen some guy trying to lead her onto the dance floor. Ledge's eyes had grown narrow, and his nostrils had flared ... right before he grabbed the guy's shoulder. He swung him around and planted his fist in the man's nose. The green-eyed monster had reared its head a few times back then. After they were married, though, the jealousy seemed to fade away. Because he had his cheatin' ways to keep him busy, she supposed. Now his focus was back on her.

A whimper escaped her lips as she realized she would not be leaving this place—unless it was willingly at his side. Or in a body bag. The horror of the situation set in. Her ribs ached as she pulled herself into a ball on the couch and continued her weeping.

Chapter 14

Chrissie headed out to see Captain Ron. She had met him on the cruise when she was at a wedding at St. Thomas over a year ago. He had talked her into applying for an entertainer position with the cruise line after he'd heard her sing at the wedding. Captain Ronald Stewart was a good friend of the groom, and Chrissie was close friends with the bride. Chrissie had since been hired, and Captain Ron had befriended her. She was thankful for that wedding gig because it had given her a new lease on life after her nasty divorce from William. But today's visit with the captain was not a pleasant one.

Chrissie had gone to Liza's suite last night and received no answer when she knocked. She had slid a note under the door, suggesting they meet for breakfast at the Lido Restaurant. She hadn't received a response to her Facebook messages using the Wi-Fi, which she assumed Liza would use to communicate with her.

Chrissie wanted to start the day out relaxed for the parasailing and zip-lining they had planned when they docked at St. Thomas today. When Liza didn't show, and Chrissie received no answer at her suite again, she made a beeline for the bridge. Something wasn't right.

Captain Ron ran into Chrissie before she made it past the pool. Quickly filling him in, he said he'd put in a call to Lucy, who handled the boarding of passengers. She would be able to tell them if Liza had indeed boarded the ship. Then they'd go from there. He promised to get back to her as soon as he heard anything.

Feeling uneasy, Chrissie went back to her cabin and waited to hear from Captain Ron. After what seemed like hours, even though it was only about one hour, Chrissie's cell phone pinged a new message through Facebook. It was Ron: *Liza was not verified to have boarded in San Juan before we set sail.*

Chrissie thanked him and set her phone down, putting her hands to her face and muttered, "What the hell is going on?" It made no sense at all. What had happened to Liza?

Chrissie snatched up her phone and started composing a quick message to Liza.

Where are you? Did you chicken out on me? I found out you didn't board. Did you miss the boarding time?

While she waited for a response, she used the Wi-Fi to look up the hotel phone number that Liza was staying at to see if she could get information that way. Chrissie cringed as she thought about what this call was going to cost her since she was "roaming." She typically just used the Wi-Fi to keep in contact with everyone back home. The front-desk clerk answered, and Chrissie asked for Liza McAllister's room. No, she didn't have the room number. The clerk flat out refused to do anything without a room number. "We do not give out any information regarding our guests. Sorry." Upset she couldn't get an answer, she opened a new Facebook message to Trinity and wrote:

Have you heard from Liza? She isn't on board. I don't know if she missed her boarding time or if she chickened out on me. And the hotel won't tell me if she's there or not. Please let me know. I've sent her several messages on FB but so far no response. And they still show unseen. Sorry to bug you at work, but this is starting to freak me out! :-/

It didn't take long for Trinity to respond:

No, I haven't heard from her. Let me know if you hear back. I'll send her a text. I hope she didn't miss her boarding! Keep me in the loop, and ditto here!

Sitting there without knowing what Liza was doing was driving her bonkers. She left her cabin and went up to the pool. It was her thinking spot when she was feeling frustrated or annoyed. Watching everyone have fun in the pool calmed her somehow. Checking her phone, she saw there was still no response from Liza. She hoped Trinity was having better luck. They should be zip-lining right now.

Someone cannonballed into the water right next to her and splashed her legs, nearly missing her phone. She got up and dried off. It was time to grab something to eat, anyway—it was close to noon. At least that would keep her busy.

As she started to walk away, her phone pinged. A message from Trinity:

Liza didn't respond when I called and left a message. And no answer from the text I sent, either. I've called Ann at work and asked to speak with Liza. She was confused and said she was on vacation this week. I apologized and said, "Oops!" Lol I didn't want to make them worry if it's nothing but her missing the boarding and she's wandering around San Juan. So, if I don't hear from her by 5 today, I'm going to call the hotel, I don't know if they'll tell me anything, but it's worth another shot. But maybe I could leave a message there. All else fails, I'll text the kids. She usually makes sure they know how to reach her when she's out. I won't let them know why. ☺

Chrissie didn't feel much better about the situation, but she knew Trinity wouldn't stop until she found Liza.

Chapter 15

The Demon pulled into Gram's long drive after driving a few miles out of his way and circling back. There had been a car that wouldn't leave his tail. He felt a little better about losing them, or rather they had turned down another route. He still felt uneasy but hadn't seen another vehicle in five minutes. He came to a stop in Gramps's shop and hit the remote to close the garage door as he grabbed all his items to take into the house. He had to check on *his wife*.

Stacking the bags in the kitchen, he fished his keys out of his pocket as he quietly walked down the hall. He softly unlocked the door, pushed it slowly forward, waiting for an attack. The only attack was on his ears. His wife was snoring. The calm returned to his blood as he washed over his wife's body with his gaze. Calm, until his eyes landed back on her left hand. His blood simmered and threatened to boil over again.

Where was his ring? His WIFE needed his RING! He looked at the floor, and then at the couch near her. He shoved the door closed behind him and hissed, "WHERE'S the RING! You NEVER take off *MY RING*!"

A frightened look cast across her tired features as his wife pulled herself into the fetal position. She wouldn't look at him. Her body was in a tight ball as he started wildly searching the couch cushions under her. Then he shifted his hands to between the cushions. The Demon roared as he brought his finger out, dripping blood. He yanked the cushion up and flung it across the small room. There! *Where the hell did a nail come from?* Lizabeth was sobbing. Her armadillo form was shaking. He pulled himself up to his full height.

"Where did you get this nail?" the Demon seethed, spittle shooting out of his mouth. "And WHAT did you do with *MY RING*?"

Lizabeth was barely audible with her face tucked in her knees.

"Louder, BITCH!" The Demon's face was red with fury.

Lizabeth raised her head, still not looking at him. "I don't know. I don't know, Ledge!" She threw her face back into the protection of her lap.

He didn't believe her. He didn't. She was lying. He started to reach for her, but something stopped him. Something inside him made him stop and think about the ring. A memory of him earlier … he had settled her back on the couch. The ring had not been there when he tucked her in. *The woods!*

The Demon stalked out of the room, slammed and locked the heavy door behind him. His eagle eyes scanned the floors on his way out of the house to find his beloved's ring. *My ring that belongs on my wife's hand!*

Chapter 16

It was killing Trinity not to have heard anything. She glanced at the clock on her computer: nearly 4 p.m. Not wanting to wait any longer, Trinity sent the twins a group text:

Hey, Laws & Lexi! I was checking in to see if your mom has sent you any pictures of her trip yet? I thought maybe you could share. I'm going through withdrawals. Lol

Lawson wrote back: *Sorry, Auntie Trinity, nothing yet. I'm sure she's wrapped up in the whole trip. I've gotta go. Lexi and I are studying for a big exam tomorrow. This prof is really a pain. <3 u*

Trinity: *Good Luck kids! ☺ <3 you both!*

Trinity now knew Liza hadn't been in touch with anyone back home. She decided to check Liza's place next. She sent a quick text to Ollie to let him know where she was headed.

Mere moments after she sent it, her cell phone rang. It was Ollie.

She answered with a simple, "Hey."

"Why are you going there so soon? I thought you didn't have to check the plants until closer to Friday?"

"Something's off. Chrissie messaged me on Facebook late this morning. Liza didn't make the boat. She didn't board. So, Chrissie asked me to do some asking around—it's easier for me to do it than her. I sent a text off to Liza. No response. The kids haven't heard from her. Her assistant hasn't seen her. Of course, they all think she's on the trip and having fun. I have a bad feeling about this. It's not like Liza. If she chickened out, she would have said something so that none of us worried."

"I'm on my way. Don't go in until I get there, and if something feels funny once you get there, just leave. Otherwise, I'll be there in five."

***

Ollie squealed into Liza's driveway, just behind his wife's car.

"What'd you do? Run red lights?" Trinity asked as she stood there, Liza's key in hand.

"I was almost home when you called. I started driving this way when I heard the tone of your voice."

"Well, I've got the key, so let's go."

Approaching the door, they both looked cautiously around. Ollie took the key from Trinity and tested the door first. It was locked. He breathed a sigh of relief. That was short-lived after he unlocked the door and they stepped into the living room. There was a mess in the kitchen. He blocked Trinity from entering, pushed her back out the door, and quietly told her to walk to the car and call 911. Trinity's face went pale, but she did as she was told.

***

"Nine-one-one, what's your emergency?"

"I, I don't know. I ..."

"Ma'am, take a breath. Please let me know where you are."

"I'm at my friend's house."

"Is anyone hurt?"

"I don't know. My friend was supposed to be gone on vacation. My husband came to help me check the house. He wouldn't let me in and told me to call you. So, I'm not sure what is happening."

"Ma'am, is your husband in any danger?"

"I don't know! I don't know what's going on!"

Ollie ran out of the house and grabbed the phone. "Operator?"

"Yes, who am I speaking with?"

"Please send the police."

"I have traced your location, and an officer has been dispatched. Is anyone hurt?"

"I don't think so, but there's been an accident inside. There's a small amount of blood on the floor. I couldn't find anyone in the house."

"Please stay where you are and don't touch anything. Can I get your name, sir?"

"Oliver Gold. Elizabeth McAllister lives here."

"Thank you, Oliver. The officer should be there momentarily. I'll hold the line while you wait."

"Thank you. Oh, wait—the patrol car is pulling up now. Thank you."

"You're welcome."

As the officer approached, Trinity wanted to ask Ollie more about what he'd seen in there but figured she'd learn it all soon enough. Her knees nearly buckled thinking about the blood Ollie had mentioned.

The tall, lanky officer unfolded himself from his patrol car and walked toward them. "Hello, I'm Officer Walker. What seems to be the problem?" Trinity immediately liked him—his face was kind, and his tone helpful.

Ollie jumped right in. "I don't know. We arrived a short while ago. The door was locked. We're here because our friend, Elizabeth McAllister, didn't get on the cruise she was supposed to board yesterday. Our other friend, Chrissie, who's on the cruise right now, called my wife—" he motioned toward Trinity "—and said she couldn't find Liza on the ship." So we came here. I stepped in first and saw the, uh, mess in the kitchen. I sent Trinity back to the car to call 911. I walked through the house and didn't find Liza. The garage is empty," Oliver finished, drawing in a deep breath after releasing all that in one fell swoop.

"Please wait here." Officer Walker drew his gun as a precaution, radioed someone, and walked into the house. In the meantime, a second officer arrived, identified himself as Sergeant Seaver as he lumbered toward them.

Ollie repeated his story and indicated Officer Walker had just entered the house. The sergeant asked about their well-being—and once they'd assured him that they were fine but very concerned, he proceeded to enter the house as well. Trinity and Ollie stayed put, arms around each other.

***

Seaver called out to Walker, letting him know he was there to assist. They cleared the house, making note that there were no broken windows or signs of forced entry. The kitchen door, which led to the back yard, however, was unlocked.

Officer Walker said, "I'm going to check the back yard. This door is unlocked, and I don't recall the man mentioning he'd gone to the back yard."

Nodding his head, Seaver knelt on the floor near the broken glass. The small pool of liquid on the floor definitely looked like blood. Standing, he stepped back and assessed the kitchen. The table was haphazardly off-center, and the chairs were knocked over. It looked like someone had shoved the table from the kitchen-door side of the room. He gingerly stepped over the glass area and headed for the door that he assumed led to the attached garage he had noticed on the house when he arrived.

Empty. No additional vehicles other than those present.

He looked around out back for a few minutes, then headed back inside. "I didn't see anything out of the ordinary upon first look. Then I checked around the windows. There are large footprints in the dirt by the windows of the master bedroom. What do you think, Sarge?"

"Yeah, this smells fishy. Blood, broken glass—maybe that's what caused the blood—but kitchen furniture is all out of whack. Something happened. We need to find out where Ms. McAllister is and get Detective Hannah over here. The two people outside are visibly concerned about their friend. I'm gonna go out there with them."

"I'll radio Hannah."

"He'll want to talk to them. I'll make sure they wait."

***

Detective Hannah had arrived on the scene and called another detective to get the search warrant started so they could get the Mobile Crime Lab there to process the scene. Walker and Seaver had already taped off the house. After Hannah had quickly introduced himself to the Golds, he headed to the house to check out the scene. He made notes as he eyeballed the entire interior as well as the back yard. Then he returned to the front yard.

He motioned to Seaver and Walker. "Let's check with the neighbors, see if anyone has heard or seen anything suspicious around here recently. The back yard has trees surrounding it like the front here, so be sure to check around the back side of this block as well. I don't know how much folks will have seen, since the driveway is pretty secluded with all the trees and vegetation. But we gotta give it a try."

Seaver and Walker left to canvas the neighborhood while an unmarked car pulled in. Detective Reyes got out with papers in his hand. "I got the warrant to search the residence and property and collect evidence. The Mobile Crime Lab has been called, and they're about half an hour out."

Hannah nodded, then turned to Oliver and Trinity Gold. The wife was leaning into her husband. Both were clearly upset. He wanted to hear what they had to say. Reyes followed.

Chapter 17

The Mobile Crime Lab began the elaborate processing of the crime scene. Collecting prints, excluding prints, placing markers, gathering evidence, the whole shebang. They started the triplicate return and tabulation form, which notated items that were taken from the premises for the case. While they worked diligently inside the house, Detective Hannah interviewed the Golds, who shared what they knew yet again.

Just as Hannah was about to wrap things up with the couple, Seaver and Walker approached with subdued faces. Hannah excused himself and pulled the officer's to the side, out of earshot of the Golds.

"You weren't gone too long. Did you either of you find something?"

"No, not too many neighbors at home to interview. We'll try again within the hour." Seaver said as he flipped through his small notepad. "The next-door neighbors on the right have never met her, though they would see her around from time to time. They said she kept to herself, a quiet person, and they didn't recall seeing anything that might be of interest in terms of what's happening here."

Hannah looked expectantly at Walker, who said, "Right. So, the neighbor across the street mentioned seeing a car pull in very early Saturday morning, but he'd gone back to bed after he got a drink of water. He wasn't sure of anything else. Said Ms. McAllister was a quiet neighbor and stayed out of his business."

Not much to work with, Hannah thought. *At least not yet.* He patted each officer on the shoulder. "Thanks. Reyes and I have this covered now. You guys need to go in and give your information and prints to the Crime Lab gurus. Then maybe check to see if any other neighbors have come home yet before heading back to the Law Enforcement Center. I know it was close to shift change when you arrived."

The two officers nodded and turned to carry out their marching orders post-haste.

Hannah called out to Reyes, who was sitting in his vehicle. "Reyes, dial LEC and issue a missing-person alert. Also, list as 'endangered' into LEIN. We need a BOLO on her vehicle, too." The Michigan Law Enforcement Information Network (LEIN) was a statewide computerized information system to aid law enforcement officers on their cases. Reyes gave Hannah the thumbs-up and started the process.

Hannah was walking back to the Golds when something occurred to him. He asked Mrs. Gold to call Liza's cell phone while they were there, hoping by chance she'd pick up this time. Liza didn't answer—it went to voicemail as before—but that wasn't the worst part. Shortly after that call, a tall, lanky lab guy brought Liza's cell phone out of the house in an evidence bag. "I heard it ringing. I found it under the couch near the kitchen." He handed it to Hannah and waited.

Trinity broke into a sob. "Liza would never leave her cell phone behind."

Oliver grabbed her as her knees gave out.

Detective Hannah knew they had to get a warrant to search Elizabeth McAllister's phone. He pointed the Lab Guy in Reyes's direction and said, "Need a warrant to search the phone. Reyes will get it." Lab Guy turned on his heel and headed toward Reyes's vehicle holding the bag out in front of him.

Reyes was on the phone for several more minutes before he called out to Hannah, "Gonna head back to the department to pick up the warrant and find the magistrate to sign it."

"It's late," Hannah said. "Good luck."

Reyes settled behind the wheel of his vehicle and took off.

***

Thankfully, Hannah didn't have to wait long for Reyes's return. The officer hopped out of his car just thirty minutes later with the papers in hand. Hannah popped an eyebrow, surprised at the quick turnaround.

"Magistrate was there signing other papers. I lucked out," Reyes said with a shrug. "I'll leave this in the house along with all the other paperwork. Maybe she'll show up soon, you know?"

Reyes, always the positive one, Hannah thought, allowing himself a small grin. And he had to admit, there was a lot of "positive" in being able to view Ms. McAllister's cell phone without restriction.

Just a minute later, Reyes was back outside with the bagged phone. He handed it to Hannah, who could hardly wait to see what he could see.

With gloved hands, he pulled the phone out and opened it. No passcode required. "Small favors," he muttered and then began to scroll through the phone.

He stopped when he realized the Golds would be helpful in identifying some of the recent calls and messages. He walked over to his car, where the Golds were tucked away so they could stay warm and calm down a bit. They weren't interested in leaving, anyway, it seemed.

"Ma'am, sir, I see the last person she called and spoke with shows only one name. Lawson. Do you know who that could be?"

"Yes, that's her son. Lawson. He has a twin sister named Alexis, and they're in their second year of college here at Northwood University," Trinity said.

"Do they all get along?"

"Oh God, yes. She loves those kids. And they love her. That's why they stayed close to home when making their choice for college."

"The other call was to Alexis—you just explained who she is. Ms. McAllister also made a recent text to you."

"Please don't call Lawson and Alexis right away, at least not until tomorrow afternoon. Lawson said they were both studying for an exam when I texted him earlier today to see if his Mom had sent him any pictures of the cruise yet—it was my way of trying to find out if they'd heard from her at all. They hadn't. I don't want them worrying, at least not until they've finished their exams," Trinity's words rushed out of her. It was the most she'd said to him so far.

"I can't guarantee anything, ma'am, but I'll do my best to see that this case is handled with the utmost respect to Ms. McAllister and her family."

Standard lingo, but it seemed to do the trick, because Trinity reached out and grabbed his arm, her face still wet with tears, and thanked him profusely. Then, new tears started flowing. Oliver pulled her close and kissed the top of her head.

When she'd calmed down a bit, he handed Detective Hannah a small piece of paper. "Here, I've written down both our numbers. I know they're in her phone already, but ... if you can stay in touch ..." He paused, obviously choking back some emotion of his own. "We're her only family, aside from the kids. Well, honorary family."

Ah, a question Hannah had yet to ask came to the front of his mind. "Where is Mr. McAllister? No one's even mentioned him. And it doesn't look like he lives on the premises." He looked from Oliver to Trinity and back to Oliver again.

Oliver cleared his throat, probably more to regain his composure than dealing with a tickle. He said, "Yes, well, they're recently divorced. His name's Ledge McAllister. He owns the marketing firm over on Waverly, McAllister Designs."

Trinity didn't say a word in response, but by her facial expression alone—narrowed eyes and pinched lips—Hannah could clearly see that she was not impressed with Ledge McAllister. He couldn't let that slip by.

"Trinity, I'm sensing by the look on your face that maybe you're not feeling so great about Mr. McAllister. Am I reading you correctly, ma'am?"

She sniffled. "Yes, you are."

"Please, fill me in."

At that point, the words really poured out of Trinity—what she thought of Ledge, what had happened in the marriage. Ollie kept trying to get his wife to tone it back some, but that wasn't happening. She was on a roll. After giving him Ledge's cell phone number, she wrapped things up by saying, "The divorce was quiet. He hasn't been around bothering her. She would have told me. He did send her flowers, trying to woo her back, a week after he got caught with his pants down. But that was the last time she heard from him, until they were in the courtroom the day of the divorce. As far as I know, he hasn't tried to reach her since. But you never know with that man. The jerk."

***

Oliver kept quiet, watching the detective as he wrote on his notepad. Thoughts ran through his head. Ledge had asked him on quite a few occasions to get Liza to talk to him during and after the divorce. It wasn't until the past two months or so that Ledge had stopped talking to him. Ollie figured Ledge had finally gotten the message that Liza was moving on and there was no point in hounding Ollie any further.

But Ollie kept that bit of information to himself. The McAllisters had been through enough, and he wasn't going to add fodder to the police report. He had no reason to believe Ledge would ever hurt Liza. Ledge still loved her; Ollie knew that.

Detective Hannah snapped his notepad shut and said, "Thank you both. I think that's all I have for now. I'll be in touch. You can head home now."

"Should we stay while they work?" Trinity looked at the house.

"No, ma'am. They'll be here quite a while. You should go home and try to get some rest."

"Come on, honey," Ollie said, leading her out of the officer's car. "Are you okay to drive?" He looked her over, concern washing through him. She looked a wreck.

But she said, "I'm okay. Really. I don't want to have to come back here tomorrow to pick up my car." She shivered, looking back at the house again.

She had a point there. They thanked the detective and headed to their respective cars. Officers had parked behind them, blocking them in, so they had to wait for Reyes to clear the way.

After tucking Trinity into her car and asking for further assurances that she would be okay behind the wheel, Ollie closed the door and headed to his own vehicle. He waited for her to back out of the drive and then followed closely behind her.

He felt as shaky as she looked. He'd never had anything like this happen before and wasn't quite sure how to handle it. But he needed to figure it out during the short drive home. His family came before his own feelings. He'd deal with his emotions later.

***

It was late enough in the evening that Trinity knew Chrissie would be working her shift. She sent a Facebook message to Chrissie, asking her to call her in the morning. She wanted to tell her all about what had happened that day, but she didn't feel up to it at the moment. Besides, Chrissie would only end up being more upset than she already was. It would be just too much for Trinity to process, as drained as she already was, emotionally and physically.

Trinity would be at work the next morning, but she could still take the call. She worked in HR for a department store in the mall, and it wasn't payroll week, so she'd have the time.

And then she questioned herself yet again—waiting until tomorrow to talk this out with Chrissie would only allow Trinity more time to sit and stew. And cry.

On cue, the tears started flowing again. She replayed all the information she had given the detective about Liza, right down to the times of her flights. But it just didn't seem like enough.

None of it was enough. Liza was missing, and no one had a damn clue about it.

***

Ollie heard his wife's sobs from his spot at the kitchen sink. He entered the living room and found her wrapped in a blanket, curled up in a chair.

"Now, now," he said, then scooped her up and took her to the couch. Their daughter, Abbie, walked in at just that time and joined them in a group hug. She knew the basics—that Liza was missing—because Ollie had made a quick call to her earlier, letting her know where they were and why. He'd insisted she made sure all the doors were locked, promising himself to call a security company tomorrow to see about an alarm. This kind of stuff didn't happen to small-town people, right?

Wrong. They were right in the thick of it.

Ollie gently held his ladies. They said a prayer for Liza. That was all they could do. It killed him not to be out there looking for her, but he had no idea where she was, who had taken her, or why. But something had definitely happened in that house—he had seen the blood on the floor. The detective had said they didn't find her purse or luggage, and her truck was gone, too.

He wanted to call Ledge but knew this would throw him off the deep end. He hoped the detective didn't release the dogs on Ledge until tomorrow. The Gold house was already in upheaval; Ollie didn't know how much more he could handle in one night.

Chapter 18

Tuesday

Chrissie finally arrived back to her cabin around 1:30 a.m. after a long set. Fishing her phone out of her purse, she tapped in the passcode. She had one message on Facebook—from Trinity. She was hoping for good news. Instead, it was no news.

Please give me a call in the morning. It doesn't matter what time. <3

She worried some more and paced her small room. Finally, after fifteen minutes of that, she nixed the idea of calling Trinity right then, since it was almost two in the morning, and instead, she decided to shower and go to bed. She set her alarm for 8 a.m.

Chrissie headed to the shower. She pulled her hair up into a messy bun and stepped into the hot water, letting the spray wash over her. She stood there for twenty minutes, trying to think what had gone wrong. So many scenarios crossed her mind: *Is Liza dead? Is she hurt? Did she chicken out? No, if she chickened out, Trinity would have sent a chicken emoji and left it at that.*

"What the hell happened to you, Liza?"

Chrissie dried off and slipped into the T-shirt she slept in. She braided her long, strawberry-blond hair and brushed her teeth. Grabbing her phone, she then messaged Trinity that she'd call a little after eight the next morning and hoped that was okay. Surprised, she got a reply before her head hit the pillow.

That will work. Talk to you then. Sleep well! <3

A sinking feeling crept into the pit of Chrissie's stomach again. This was not good. Apparently, Trinity wasn't sleeping, either. She clicked the light off at her bedside and rolled over to try to get comfortable. Thoughts were racing. *Something bad has happened.* "Please be alive, Liza, please!"

Praying for her friend, she rolled back over and turned her nightstand radio on, switched it to the sound of rushing water, and tried again to get comfortable. She set the play time for sixty minutes and hoped that was long enough. Her mind took her to pictures of a car crash, then an airplane crash.

She smacked the bed with her fists and turned the volume up a little to help drown out her thoughts.

Somewhere in the midst of her mental turmoil, her body gave in, and she finally slept for a few hours.

***

Trinity was at her desk when the phone rang on Tuesday at 8:07 a.m. She had barely slept at all and felt anything but refreshed. Soon, she would be telling Chrissie all about the "nothing" they knew so far about Liza's disappearance. She let out a deep sigh, knowing it was Chrissie on the other end of that line. "Payroll, this is Trinity."

"Trin! What's going on?" Chrissie sounded like she had run a marathon.

"Hi, Chris." Trinity paused and took a deep breath, "I'll start from the last time we spoke. I haven't been able to reach Liza. I texted Lawson, using the excuse of wanting vacation pictures, and he hadn't heard from her. The twins were studying hard for exams, so I haven't bothered them since." She paused and heard Chrissie inhale and release it through her nose. Trinity continued. "That was about four o'clock yesterday. Then I decided to head to Liza's and see if she was there. I texted Ollie and told him I was going over there, and then he called me and asked me what was going on. I filled him in, and he met me at Liza's. He took the key from me and went inside, but before he would let me in, he told me to ..." Trinity dropped off and grabbed a tissue.

"Trin? Trinity, are you still there?" Chrissie was panicked.

"Yes." Trinity tried to calm herself and then proceeded to tell Chrissie the rest of the story.

"Fuck!" Chrissie was swearing a shit storm through sobs. She had always had a mouth on her when things went awry. This time, Trinity couldn't blame her one bit. "What do we do now? I don't know how to handle this, being this far away from everyone."

"Chris, breathe, just breathe. We can't lose it now. We have to pray for Liza. That's all we can do right now. The police are working on this. If I hear from her or the police, you'll be the first to know. I promise I'll find a way to let you know immediately. For now, just breathe…" Trinity felt calmer, now in mother mode, trying to get Chrissie's stress meter outside of the red zone.

"Okay—" Chrissie breathed hard, in and out, in and out "—okay. I still have some of my anxiety pills left. I'll take one of those. I know we need to be strong. I feel so alone right now out here. This cruise can't be over fast enough. I barely slept. I'm … a mess! How am I supposed to sing tonight, Trin? I—"

Trinity interrupted her. "You'll be fine. I know you. Once you put your gown on, it'll be like putting on your cheerleading uniform. You'll be in work mode, and nothing will stop you from performing. You got this; you always have."

"Okay, okay. But … okay, so I'm feeling panicked. What if she isn't found? What if that blood was hers? What if …?"

"Chris! You need to stop those bad thoughts. Just pray. That's all you need to focus on right now. I don't want you alone today. Are you able to spend time with the captain or some of the other entertainers?"

"Yes, yes, I can do that. I'll call Kyle. He and the other comedians always lift my spirits. I'll get ready and go find them. They should be up soon."

"Great. I love you, Chrissie. Stay focused on the tasks today. I promise if I hear anything, you'll be the first one I call."

"Love you, Trin. Please, please keep in touch."

"Will do, Strawberry Shortcake." Trinity used the nickname she'd given her back in high school. That brought a little chuckle from Chrissie.

"Cute, *Blondie*," Chrissie said.

Now it was Trinity's turn to let loose a chuckle. They said their goodbyes and went back to their worrying.

Chapter 19

Tuesday

With Reyes at his side, Detective Hannah stood in front of the McAllister twins in the cramped dorm room, watching their response to his declaration of the missing person. Hannah had started with the fact that Lawson was the last person to have verbal contact with his mother via her cell phone. Lawson broke down completely. Alexis seemed to be handling it better, but only because she was trying to console her twin brother.

After a few minutes of processing the news, the twins looked expectantly at the officers. Tears shone in their eyes and streaked their faces, but they were quiet now. Detective Hannah went directly into what law enforcement knew, what had been done thus far, and what steps were still to be taken, which included interviews. Like this one, now, in the dorm room.

Like the seasoned detective that he was, he kept up with his pointed approach but mixed it with a dose of gentleness and compassion. The mix was important. *You get more flies with honey than vinegar*, he reminded himself. If *there were any flies to be had in this situation.*

The questions flowed out of him:

Had they heard from their mother?

Where were they on Saturday? And the past few days?

Who were they with?

The twins responded to each question almost in unison, knowing each other like the back of their own hands. Nothing overtly concerning, Hannah noted. Then he asked the last two questions.

How had the divorce gone down between their parents? Could their dad somehow be involved in this?

The twins, who had easily answered the prior questions, were suddenly shocked out of any complacency they may have been feeling.

Lawson said defiantly, "Dad loved Mom. He would never hurt her."

Alexis nodded. "Dad didn't like that they were getting a divorce, but he still loved her. He made a mistake, that's all. With that woman and stuff. Mom didn't want to talk about it, so we let them heal on their own."

Lawson repeated, "Dad would never hurt Mom."

And with that, Hannah and Reyes saw that the meeting was going nowhere else. Hannah thanked them, and they left. They were heading back to the department in silence, both lost in thought.

With Reyes behind the wheel, Hannah finally took out his cell and dialed the Saginaw sheriff's office. He needed to touch base with them to see what they had found out at the MBS Airport in Freeland. They were contracted to do security for the airport. Reyes had emailed them a copy of Ms. McAllister's license earlier in the morning to check on the flight she was supposed to be on. Hannah had already called the hotel in San Juan himself, and there was no record of her checking in at all. He hadn't bothered trying to call the cruise line's menagerie of madness to get to the right person. Besides, Trinity had mentioned that Liza had not boarded the ship—this according to Chrissie, who was actually on board and had checked.

No, he would wait and save himself that headache until after he heard what the airport findings were. If she'd not taken a flight out of MBS as planned, then he would focus more on the local area than her vacation plans. MBS Airport was under the Saginaw County Sheriff Department jurisdiction. Any information for surveillance would have to come from them.

Hannah left a message for the Saginaw County sheriff to call him back. She wasn't in the office. He hoped they had some of the evidence back from the rush he had put on the case. He also knew how backlogged everything was. Hannah placed his phone in his pocket; he knew his chances of having any results back this soon were zero to zilch. Timing was everything in a missing-person case, and this one was not moving fast enough.

Chapter 20

Ledge had been busy this morning, putting in new double-sided dead bolts on all the doors. These locks required a key on both sides of the door to enter and exit the house. The old wooden windows were swollen shut from non-use and age, so he didn't waste his time and money on locks for those. Ledge was now able to allow Lizabeth to roam if she so wanted to, now that the house was sealed tighter than Fort Knox. *This is for my peace of mind; you won't be able to escape now, my little tiger.*

He actually didn't remember purchasing the locks, but he remembered checking on Lizabeth after he had arrived home. She had been snoring softly when he peeked in on her—after first making sure she wasn't looming next to the door, waiting to pounce at him. He hated that he'd lost his temper again. It made him crazy that he couldn't remember what happened whenever he did. "I should have listened to you, Lizabeth. I should have found someone to help me, other than that quack doctor I'd tried. If you work with me, I promise I will get help," he muttered to himself.

Ledge wandered the house and checked the doors and windows six times. It was now five in the afternoon. He threw a quick meal together, calming his nerves. *Time to get Lizabeth.* Walking down the hall, he pulled the key from his pants pocket and unlocked the door, standing back a bit in case she charged. Lizabeth was still lying on the couch, sleeping. He approached slowly. He tapped her foot and tickled it. He smiled to himself; he knew her body like the back of his hand. And her ticklishness was her Kryptonite. Yanking her foot back, her eyes flew open, and she moaned and clutched her ribs.

Wanting to console her, he said, "Can you take a deep breath, Liza-bear? I can wrap your ribs if you want." He vaguely remembered putting

ACE bandages away in the bathroom. *Damn, I have definitely faded in and out today.*

"No, I can breathe. Only bruised." She hissed the words through her clenched teeth. He knew she was in pain, but his stubborn tiger wouldn't admit it.

"Okay, are you hungry? I made supper if you'd like to join me in the kitchen."

Her stomach summoned an angry howl at the mention of a meal, and she nodded. "I need to go to the bathroom first." Slowly getting up, she checked herself before trying to stand. She looked wobbly. Ledge moved in and picked her up. He then deposited her in the bathroom, waited until she regained her balance, stepped outside, and closed the door. Standing in the hallway, he heard her flush and wash her hands before she opened the door.

He escorted her to the kitchen. She seemed okay, but her legs were still rubbery. He attributed that to not eating. He blamed himself for that. He should have made her something to eat earlier. Or had he? His memory of today was hazy at best. He shook his head to clear the cobwebs.

"Everything is ready."

"Thanks."

She wasn't smiling. She wasn't happy, but she didn't seem pissed off. He had a hard time reading her. She'd regressed, and that was his fault. He knew he shouldn't have taken things so fast.

She sat at the island, silent with her plate of food in front of her.

"What would you like to drink? I have all the usual suspects in the fridge." He stopped and looked her over again, "I should get you some pain pills."

Her voice came out monotone. "Pain pills with water is fine. Thanks."

"I'll be right back. Stay seated." He pulled a water bottle from the fridge and then slid it toward her as he passed on his way to the bathroom. He returned in short order and handed her the pills, which she dutifully swallowed.

Lizabeth didn't even look up as she arranged her plate and began eating. Things had relapsed tremendously, and it was his entire fault. *You dumb SOB, Ledge! You had her Sunday night, and you messed it up!* Ledge tried to remember yesterday afternoon, but he failed. He only remembered finding the bag of locks on the counter that morning when he woke up. He knew they'd eaten a late supper, too, because of the dishes in the dishwasher.

Trying not to appear too overbearing, he stopped staring at her and slid into the chair next to hers at the island. They ate in silence. Time passed as Ledge tried to figure out where he'd gone wrong to make her want to leave after the pleasant time they'd had Sunday evening. He became so lost in his own thoughts that he hadn't realized Lizabeth was on the other side of the kitchen, rinsing her plate in the sink. He jumped up and quickly was standing next to her.

"Here, let me get this. You need your rest. If you like, you can take Gram's room. I won't bother you."

"Thanks."

Liza wandered down the hallway, and he trailed behind at a quiet pace to make sure she didn't lose her balance. She was better now that she'd eaten. *Thank God.* Ledge stood in the hall until he heard Gram's door click shut. He turned back down the hall toward the kitchen and started the cleanup. What would he do to occupy himself now? His Gramps's shop came to mind, but he shook his head. *No, I don't want to leave Lizabeth alone in the house any more than she already has been.*

Looking around the kitchen, he was satisfied that everything was in its place, so he wandered to the living room. He turned on the lights and saw his family photos hanging on the wall. Not wanting to lose his composure, he spun around, and his eyes landed on the cabinet under the TV. That was where Gram kept some old photo books.

"Do you really want to walk down that road of sadness today?"

He really needed to stop talking to himself. After Lizabeth had left him, he'd picked up that nasty habit. One day while walking into the gym, he noticed people nearby backing away from him cautiously like he was crazy. It was then he realized he had said something out loud. Ledge shook that memory away. He scanned the room, and his eyes landed on the end table by the couch. Gram had kept her knitting in there, and it was an easy spot for her to hide it away if someone stopped by.

She was a neat freak.

"Everything has a place and should be in its place when not in use." Gram's old saying replayed in his mind like a broken record so many years ago until he had made it his habit.

Ledge knelt down on one knee near the couch, pulled the little door open, and peeked inside. There was an old project of hers still on her knitting needles. Ledge sat down cross-legged on the floor and pulled it out to examine it. Gram had shown him how to knit many, many moons ago. He hadn't had much interest in it, but it was something he could do with her, so he'd let her show him how. He wondered if this was something he could finish—having something of hers that they both had worked on would be nice.

He found the pattern under all the yarn. It was for a baby blanket. This stopped Ledge cold. Gram had passed away shortly after he and Lizabeth were married. They hadn't finished college yet. Gram must have been planning ahead, because Liza definitely wasn't pregnant at that time. He sucked in a breath to keep the tears away and whispered, "Oh, Gram, I'll finish this for you."

He knew enough not to disturb her project until he retrained himself how to knit. He put the knitting back in its place and vowed to finish it at a later date. Maybe he could give it to his first grandchild. That thought brightened his mood. His mind then wandered to Gram's craft room. He walked down the hall to his room and entered the closet. He hadn't shown Lizabeth the hidden door in there. He slid the clothes back and opened the craft-room door. Prior to this being Gram's craft room, it was his and his brother's secret playroom. Gramps had put that together for them when they were very young. He and John had one of those old race tracks set up in there, and they played with it all the time when they visited. It was their special place.

Ledge often came into the craft room when he was missing John. In fact, Gram had found him in here shortly after John's death—Ledge had thought that maybe his brother was hiding. After all these years, he still couldn't believe his brother was gone.

It wasn't long after that, Gram asked him to help her move things around. She wanted a fresh start for him. So, he helped her swap rooms with him. The room that he had placed Lizabeth in when he'd first brought her here was originally Gram's craft room. Gram had changed rooms and had taken over their secret playroom. *Time doesn't wait for anyone to heal. It keeps moving.*

And then his parents died.

He turned abruptly, no longer wanting to remember the pain of his agonizing childhood. Closing the door and putting the clothes back in place, he headed out of his room to check on Lizabeth. He slowly opened the door when he didn't hear anything. He walked to the edge of the bed and listened. The light from the hall shone on Lizabeth, and he could see her chest rising and falling at a steady rate. Feeling relieved, he went to the chair next to the bed so he could watch her sleep—his favorite past time. He let his mind wander while he listened to her cute little snore.

Chapter 21

Mid-July

The divorce was final, and Ledge felt as low as a person could feel. He paced his friend's garage floor, searching for answers to his woes—from Ollie, from inside himself, from anywhere. He didn't want to believe it was too little too late. But that's pretty much what Ollie was telling him.

"Ledge, you need to let Liza go," Ollie said. "I know it hurts like hell, man, but you can't keep beating a dead horse."

Ledge shook his head. "I know I fucked up big time, but I need her. I can't breathe without her!" He held back tears as he raked his hands through his hair. "I need to see her! I ... can't say goodbye." He turned and looked at Ollie with tears in his eyes. "I *need* her."

"Dude, I get it. I'd feel as torn up as you if I lost Trinity. But I can't fix this. Liza is firm on her choice. Trinity would have my hide on a pole if I even tried to mention some sort of reconciliation to Liza. I love you like a brother, but I can't help you out of this. Not this time. It's done. Just let her be."

Ledge said nothing.

Ollie shook his head and looked Ledge right in the eye, placed his hands on his shoulders. "Focus on yourself right now, man. Maybe find a doctor, some professional to talk to. I mean, we both know you haven't been the same since you started taking that Cantril. And now all this with the divorce ... Get some fresh advice ..." Ollie's voice trailed off as he let go of Ledge's shoulders and stepped away. Now it was him who was pacing. "Maybe, just maybe, Liza will see you're serious and ... Okay, that's a long shot, man. I can't sugarcoat this. You broke her heart, dude. And I hate you for that in a way—two of my best friends are hurting because of it."

Damn it, Ollie, you're not helping! Ledge didn't want to see any more doctors. He only wanted his wife back. *Ex-wife.* He grimaced and hung his head. Just the word made his heart sink in despair. No, he didn't need "professional help," but maybe if he tried to make an effort, and Liza happened to hear about it … yeah, maybe then she'd want to talk to him. Reconsider. Yeah, that's what he needed to do. He could pull that off. He was the master of his castle. He could do anything he set his mind to. He looked up at Ollie and said, "I'll put it in motion—get some doctorly advice. I want her back, and if you think this will help, even if it's a long shot, I'll do it."

"That's great, man!" Ollie grinned as he splayed his hands. "I'll ask around tomorrow for a good doctor."

"No, man, I can do this. I need to do this on my own. It won't work if she finds out you set something up for me."

"Cool. Good thinking. Keep me in the loop. I'm here for you, buddy."

"I know you are. You've been my savior more times than I can count." Ledge slapped his pal on the shoulder a few times.

"Hey, you covered my butt enough times. I've got your back."

"I know. I know." Ledge nodded. "So, where's Trinity tonight? I don't want to overstay my welcome if she's about to come back."

"No, you're good, she's out … uh, with some friends." Ollie internally smacked himself for almost spilling the beans about Liza and the girls going out on the town, celebrating her divorce from Ledge.

Ledge perceptively caught the quick pause and realized who Trinity was out with. That meant they were probably at their favorite club. Ledge tipped his whiskey back, finishing the drink in one gulp, covering the smile that had started creeping up his lips. He would wrap things up here, maybe pretend to receive an important text, and then head to the club.

He turned away from Ollie to hide his smile as he walked over to the makeshift bar. "Need a refill, buddy?"

"Sure, I'll take one more," Ollie said. He held out his glass, and Ledge poured some more for the both of them.

"Oh." Ledge set the whiskey bottle down and reached into his pocket to pull out his cell. Glanced down, did his best frowny face, and said, "Thanks for the talk. But I need to take care of this. Sorry I have to cut this short." He picked up his glass and poured the golden liquor down his throat.

Ollie did the same. "No problem. Keep me posted on any new developments."

"Will do. Thanks for all the help tonight," Ledge said he headed out. He let the smirk fully form as he all but raced to his car.

***

Ledge was walking toward the club door when the girls flew out of the building. *What luck!* He stopped, slipped back in between two cars, and squat-walked behind the vehicles to hide himself. They were headed in his direction at a fast pace.

"OMG!" Chrissie yelled. "That was crazy!"

"Get to the car!" Trinity hollered, pushing Chrissie and reaching behind her for Liza's hand.

Ledge watched as Lizabeth brought up the rear—*and what a rear it is.* She looked so good. Ledge almost gave his position away when he rose up to watch her. He dropped back down and followed close behind, using the row of vehicles as his cover. He watched them climb into a red convertible.

"Gotcha!" Ledge whispered, and a huge Grinch grin splayed across his face as he noticed he had parked just two vehicles away from them. He slipped into his car and backed out as they were reaching the street.

He stayed one car behind them, maintaining an eagle eye so he didn't lose them. Lizabeth and the girls were oblivious to his pursuit. They never looked back after leaving the club. *Should be more cautious, ladies.*

Ledge was so intent on following them that he'd lost track of where he was. The car ahead of him put on the brakes, and then he saw the shiny red car pull into a hidden driveway. Ledge passed the driveway slowly; it was another bar, just outside of town.

Ledge made a loop, backtracked to the bar, and pulled in, noticing Chrissie's car was empty. They had parked on the far end. He headed to the back of the building to park his car so they didn't see it. Had he had time to plan, he'd have rented a car to further his cover. But that wasn't how things rolled out—so be it.

Satisfied with his hiding spot, he sauntered toward the front of the building. But how to enter without being obvious? Just as he rounded the corner, he saw another couple about to enter. He couldn't believe his luck. He quick-stepped to catch up to them so he could hide behind the mountain of a man and his lady as they walked into the bar.

Ledge peeked out around the couple and caught sight of the girls. They'd taken a table on the opposite side of the bar, close to the dance floor. He snuck down the side wall to the back corner booth, which was thankfully vacant, and slid into it, hiding in the shadows. He had the perfect vantage point to keep an eye on his beautiful bride—*to hell with that divorce! She'll always be my bride.* The waitress sashayed up to the table and leaned in, hanging her voluptuous bosom in his line of sight, "What'll ya have?"

"Whiskey, neat."

"Be right back, honey." She winked, then turned and let her hips propel her across the floor.

Ledge had no interest in her. At one time, he would have had her number by the end of the night and taken her home when her shift was over. Not tonight. His focus was seven tables away, and she was headed for the dance floor. Ledge was so captivated with Lizabeth dancing, he didn't even acknowledge the waitress when she brought his drink to the table. He could watch Lizabeth all night. She was smiling and having a blast. He realized that he hadn't seen her that happy in … a long time. Clouds were starting to form around him, but he pushed them back. Now was not the time to draw attention to himself.

He had tried to follow Lizabeth home several times to see where she was staying, but she'd either spotted him or his dumb luck had left him losing her in traffic. Tonight he wasn't going to lose her. He was going to make sure of that. He relaxed back into the booth. The whiskey on the table was calling his name, but he left it there. *No clouds tonight.*

Chapter 22

Present Day

Ledge lifted himself slowly so as not to wake his sleeping princess and silently strode from the bedroom, closing the door behind him. He figured he should check his work email and phone. He had forgotten he'd stashed it in Gram's craft room to keep it out of Lizabeth's reach—and to avoid distractions. But he needed to make sure there was nothing serious that had sprung up with his business this week. His coworkers would get suspicious if he waited too long to respond to any major issues.

Ledge powered up his cell, and it immediately started ringing after the start-up screen disappeared. He startled, nearly dropping it on the floor. Fumbling with the phone, he finally silenced the ringer before it rang a third time.

He shouldn't be receiving any calls. He had told everyone to email him if they needed him, or text "911" it if it was an emergency. His story was that he would be traveling out of state for a few days to drum up new clientele.

His phone dinged, indicated a voicemail was waiting for him—from his son.

"Shit!" He pulled up Lawson's message and listened.

"Dad, I don't know if you've heard or not, um ... I didn't want to leave this in a voicemail, but Mom's missing. I don't know what to do. Lexi and I are going nuts. Please call me right back, no matter what time it is, okay? We probably won't sleep tonight, anyway, so we plan to head home. I know you're on the road with work, but we want to be home. Love ya, Dad."

Shit! Shit! Shit! This is not good. How'd they find out? No one should know she's missing. He thought for a few minutes. The house. Had he left anything lying around that might stick out to the kids as strange? No. He was sure he had not. The plans for Gram's house were with him here in the craft room, and no one at home knew about this place. He was safe. He'd never had the deed changed over from his grandparents' names.

To buy some time with the kids, he sent a text off to Lawson:

Sorry I missed you, son. I will call you at home tomorrow morning. You both get some sleep. I can't get away right now. Things are going better than I'd hope for, and this meeting is headed into a late evening. I'm sure your mom is fine. You know how she likes to take time for herself and doesn't always check in. I'm getting called back into the meeting. Talk in the morning. Love, Dad

Chapter 23

Liza roused from her sleep coma. Her mouth felt like a desert wasteland. She still felt groggy, but something had awoken her. Banging from somewhere in the house? It was muffled, but clear enough. She moved toward the door in the darkness and rammed her toe into the dresser. "Ouch!" she yelped and then slapped her hand over her mouth.

Steadying herself, she walked a little more carefully and found the light switch. She almost flipped it on but thought better of it, just in case. She felt the wall until she found the doorjamb and slid her hand down to the doorknob. She turned it and slowly opened the door.

The sound was a little louder now but not much. She stuck her head into the hall to hear better and maybe see something that could explain the noise.

The hall was not lit, but the light in the kitchen left a dim glow in the hallway. She cautiously started down the hall and then remembered she wasn't wearing shoes. She went back to the room Ledge had locked her in earlier, and she found her sneakers at the end of the couch. She put them on and laced them up, all the while wondering what the noise was, what it could mean. Was she in further danger?

She made her way into the kitchen and listened again. The noise seemed to be coming from outside the house. She shuffled to the living room and looked around. The lamp on the far end table was on, but Ledge was nowhere to be seen.

Bang. Bang.

Her thoughts refocused on the noise. She went to the living room window and pulled the dusty curtains aside, which caused her to squeak out a sneeze. It was pitch black, save for a light coming from the shop door. *So, that's where he is.*

Her nerve endings got a super charge. *He's occupied. I need to leave now.*

Liza swiftly ran through the kitchen to the back door. This time, she planned to make her way around to the front of the house from the back yard, and then she would go south and hopefully find the driveway. She quickly stepped back and opened the drawer where the flashlight had been previously and breathed a sigh of relief when she saw he had stashed it back in its place. *Old habits die hard for that man.*

She flicked it on; it worked. She slipped through the mudroom, unlocked the door, and pulled, but her hand slipped off the handle. She fell backward a step. She tried again. The door wouldn't open. *What the hell?* She inspected the door and saw the problem: a shiny new dead bolt, which needed a key.

Liza ran back through the kitchen and made a beeline to the front door. Flashlight in hand, she came to a dead stop when she saw a duplicate new lock on the front door, too. About in tears, she sailed through sliding doors of the dining room. Shining her flashlight on the French doors on the west wall, she found fresh locks there, too.

New locks. All the same. All requiring keys that she didn't have.

She stood there, breathing heavily, doing her best not to completely break down. Now was not the time for a panic attack. Ledge was outside, and the banging had ... stopped. *Wait…what? Shit!*

Liza slid the dining room doors shut, raced back to the kitchen, and put the flashlight back in the drawer, careful to place it in exactly the same position. At least she hoped it was. Then she raced back to the outside door, and turned the little button on the knob to lock it. She pulled the mudroom door shut behind her, and prayed everything was in its place. No sooner had she taken one deep breath than she heard the front door opening. *He's ba-ack!*

She quickly slipped over to the fridge and fished out a bottle of water, trying to get her breathing slowed. Her heart was hammering in her chest, and she didn't have time to run back and feign sleep. She was trapped in the kitchen.

"Thirsty?" Ledge asked from behind her.

Slowly turning, she nodded, trying to gauge his mood. "Yes."

"Glad to see you that you're up. I wasn't sure whether or not to wake you. You seemed to be dead to the world when I looked in on you earlier." He grabbed a bottle of water for himself and guzzled it, then threw the container in the trash can.

"I don't think I've slept that hard in a long time," Liza said, noticing the perspiration on Ledge's forehead.

"Good. Hopefully, you're feeling rested." With an optimistic look on his face, he said, "I made cookie brownies for dessert earlier, if you're hungry."

"Not right now. I'm still a little groggy from sleeping."

"No worries. We can have it later."

She couldn't tell if he was pissed or calm. Her radar was off after almost getting caught trying to escape—again. She waited to see what his next move would be.

"Are you too awake to go back to sleep? We could play a game. The TV doesn't have anything but the regular channels. And the picture isn't that great. Gram didn't have any VHS or DVD players, so I can't offer that."

"Okay. I guess we could play a game." Liza felt uneasy. He was playing things too casually considering what had happened yesterday. She had been stuck in that room—*Gram's* room—for most of the day, sleeping on and off.

And he had been watching her sleep, too. From beneath her thick eyelashes, as she pretended to be asleep, she could see him standing over her, staring at her. His eyes were dark and unseeing, and she knew the Demon was there. She never knew when that evil bastard would show up.

Tonight, however, she saw the Ledge of old. The one she had fallen in love with—calm and reserved—was now staring at her.

"Shall we go down the hall and get the games?" he asked.

"Right, yes."

Ledge walked around the island and headed toward his room. He didn't even try to touch her. He was ten feet in front of her, and she followed on high alert. The ache was back in her ribs and her body. The pain from the bruises was pronounced, but her edginess was too strong to bother Ledge for pills. She didn't want to numb the pain, dull her senses. She needed to stay focused.

At the closet door, Ledge stepped aside, allowing her to choose a game. She grabbed the backgammon box with its musty smell, and they headed back to the kitchen.

"Do you want anything else to drink?" he asked pleasantly.

"I'll grab another water. Do you want another one, too?"

"Yes, please."

Here we go again. That sinking feeling was returning to Liza's stomach; her hackles were up. *Need to focus and not break this fragile ice. Again.* She pulled two bottles of water out of the fridge. She saw the clock on the microwave read 12:30 a.m. *This is going to be another long night. God, please help me get out of this alive.* She reluctantly returned to the table and slumped down in the chair across from Ledge. Took the top off the bottle and chugged down half of the water. Then she looked at Ledge, who had not touched his water.

"Go ahead and roll first," she said.

Ledge picked up the dice and rolled. Liza saw the dice land on the board, and her mind took her back to the time they had played this game in high school. Her haunted memories of them as a happy couple made her stomach churn with disgust. She was still reeling from everything that had happened between them this year, and here he was, sitting across from her as if nothing had happened at all. As if he hadn't caught her running for her life. Liza sat paralyzed with fear as she watched emotions dance on Ledge's face.

The shiny new locks invaded her thoughts, making her want to cry out. Knowing she was stuck in this House of Hell was starting to eat at her insides. Her skin was crawling, and she squelched the urge to scratch. Her right hand absently started spinning the heavy, loose ring on her finger. She'd lost weight, and it didn't fit as tight as it used to.

The ring had almost been her end earlier. She didn't know where he had found it or when he had slipped into her cage and put it back on her hand. She had passed out at some point after the altercation. She'd never felt that kind of fear before. Her fingers worked the ring 'round and 'round under the table. She would make sure she didn't lose that ring again.

***

Ledge looked at Lizabeth while she moved her pieces. She could have knocked him to the bar, but she didn't. This was not how she had played backgammon in the past. She was typically a ruthless player. She was testing him. She kept looking at him, waiting for something. *She's waiting for the Demon to take over, you idiot.* Ledge had gone out and banged on an old piece of equipment Gramps had in the barn. It was broken anyway, and he needed to release some energy before the Demon showed up again. He had succeeded in keeping his treacherous mood at bay. That call from his son had almost brought forth the Demon, and he hoped his reply via text hadn't alerted Lawson to anything.

His son was quick at picking up on things. Both his kids—*their* kids, rather—were smart. Lawson was studying for a finance degree, like his mom, and Alexis was studying marketing. She liked what her dad did and had been interested enough to want to go to work with him during her high school years.

He breathed a heavy sigh, which drew attention from Lizabeth, but she quickly averted her eyes. So much work he had to do to get those eyes to shine with love for him again. He hoped he had enough time. He needed to break the silence.

"I'm hungry. Are you?" he asked.

"Sure. How about those brownies?"

Ledge grabbed some plates and forks while she cut the brownies. Once settled back at the table, they took a few moments to enjoy the dessert. He looked at the dice. Had he rolled last?

"It's your roll," he suggested.

"Thanks."

This was ridiculous. These little polite sentences were driving him nuts. The silence was ringing in his head. He looked up at Lizabeth and decided to go for broke. "I'm sorry. I don't know what I did to make you leave, but I'm sorry." Seeing her stunned expression and not waiting for a verbal response, he plunged forward before he lost his nerve. "I have been doing a lot of thinking, and I wished I had listened to you about seeing someone about my problem after taking Cantril. I realize now that was a mistake. I never like to admit I'm not perfect. This is not easy for me, but I want you,

Lizabeth. You're my lifeline. I can't live without you. Whatever I did, I'm sorry."

Ledge took a breath and waited. *If you only knew how many sleepless nights I've had since you left.*

Chapter 24

Liza was floored. He'd actually apologized. This tipped her axis. She had no idea what to say. She sat there contemplating what her response should be. What would be safest, smartest? She saw by the look in his eyes that he was getting impatient with her. She could hear the clock in the kitchen ticking off the seconds.

Finally, she blurted out, "Thank you. I am at a loss. I'd wanted you to seek help for so long. You don't know what it does to me to see you lose control when that demon shows up. You're not you, Ledge. You're not you when that happens. I've been thankful the kids never got to see it." Drawing a few breaths, she continued. "I'm certain someone can help you find the Ledge I fell in love with. The real you. We can go home and start looking tomorrow." Liza said a little prayer that Ledge didn't catch on to her real goal of that last sentence.

Ledge looked at her with a blank expression. She held her breath because this was when he usually lost control. She was ready to bolt. She might be able to reach the knife drawer before he caught her; she hoped. She'd been blunt, hadn't said anything about staying with him. She wanted him to know he needed to focus on getting well, not their marriage.

She wasn't sure if that could ever be repaired after she'd seen him banging that young woman. She couldn't un-see it. Still, this moment was an opportunity to once again discuss his anger, the Demon that had started with that damn Cantril. The medicine made him dangerous, and she knew she certainly wasn't out of the woods yet. *Literally, not out of the woods.* Liza watched Ledge with trepidation, though she hoped it wasn't obvious.

"So, you're saying you want to help me get help?"

"Yes, I will help you find the help you need. I want to see you get well, Ledge."

"And once I get well, you'll move back in with me?"

"We can work on us, but you have to fix the Demon first."

"Okay." He paused, nodding. "Okay, I will do that. I'll make that my priority in the morning."

"Thank you, Ledge." Not wanting to push her luck, she didn't ask again about leaving. Something lurked beneath that facade of his, and she didn't want to bring it to the surface. Not being able to get a single exit door open scared the living daylights out of her, but she needed to stay calm so *he* would stay calm. Liza wiped her sweaty palms on her pants. Ledge might want to fix himself for Liza's sake, but the Demon probably had other plans.

He picked up the dice and rolled, then made his move on the board. He was close to winning, and she was going to let that happen. He needed a win, even if it wasn't earned.

In the end, he indeed won, but she could see from his expression that he was skeptical.

They packed the game away, and Ledge silently walked down the hall to put it back in the closet. She sat there, not knowing what to do. She was on pins and needles, fearing time was running out on this little fake-happily-married-couple routine.

When Ledge reappeared from the hall and headed for the empty dessert plates, Liza shot up from her chair. "I got these. You look tired, Ledge. Let's call it a night."

"Yes, I'm really tired all of a sudden. Thanks. Did you want to sleep in Gram's room again tonight?"

"That would be nice if it's okay with you."

He shrugged. "I'm okay with it." He walked away, and she could hear him enter the bathroom and close the door.

Liza blew some stray hair from her eyes, then got busy loading the dishwasher and putting away the brownies. When she turned around, Ledge was standing at the entrance to the kitchen. A black cloud seemed to be hanging over him. His eyes were hazy, and he was staring at her. Liza startled, stepped back, and immediately felt pinned against the sink. She cleared her throat, getting ready to say something, but every comment that popped into her head was a loaded one. She didn't want to ask if everything was all right.

Then, as silently as he had come, he walked away again.

"Goodnight, Ledge," she said.

He muttered, "Goodnight."

Liza grabbed the sponge and wiped down the countertop and the table, all the while glancing back at the spot where Ledge had just stood. Everything was already clean, but she needed something to keep her hands busy. Would he show up again? The look on his face was one she had never seen before. A chill ran through her body. She didn't know why, but she felt like something bad was going to happen ... soon.

She had to get out of there. And fast. She had to find a key to one of the dead bolts. Surely, he had an extra hidden somewhere. There was always an extra. She'd wait until she heard him sleeping, and then she'd do some snooping tonight. She glanced at the ominous ticking clock. *Correction: this morning.* It was nearly 2 a.m.

She shuffled toward the bathroom. Ledge had left his bedroom door open, and she saw he was in bed but couldn't tell which way he was facing. She turned into the bathroom and quietly shut the door. Her ribs were still aching. She grabbed the pill bottle and shook two out, then stuck her head under the faucet and washed them down.

Liza quickly disrobed, pulled her hair up into a tie, and got in the shower to wash off the day's dirtiness. She waited for the hot water to ease her muscles, and then she scrubbed down and stood there for a few more minutes, enjoying the heat. When Liza finally pulled the curtain back, she nearly jumped out of her skin.

Sitting there on the toilet, with the same emotionless expression, was Ledge.

She shakily wrapped a towel around herself and waited. Many thoughts ran through her head about how to escape this small room without him catching her first. None of them ended well. The relaxation feeling that the hot shower had given her was now replaced with the icy grip of fear. She couldn't move.

"You didn't tell me you love me. You didn't say, 'Love ya, Ledge.'"

"I ... I'm sorry, I didn't realize you were waiting for me to say it. I thought you knew." Her skin was crawling with goose bumps.

"I guess I need to hear it. I need to know I haven't lost your love, Lizabeth. I need to know you still love me. I need to hear you say it. It's been too long."

"I ... I understand. I do love you, Ledge. I do." She prayed it sounded more sincere than she felt.

He blew out a breath as he swiped a hand over his face. "Thank you. I Love you, too. You're my world, Liza-bear. Please don't give up on me. On us."

And without another word, he stood and left the room.

She tamped back the scream that was building in her body. Her teeth started to chatter from the chill he'd left in the steamy bathroom. She wasn't going to fall asleep any time soon. Now more than ever, she was driven to find that key and get the hell out of that house.

Chapter 25

Ledge sat in the chair in his dark room, where she couldn't see him watching her in the bathroom. He had left the door open on purpose when he walked out. He had wanted to touch her when she was in the shower. Wanted to pull her close to him and feel her body heat against his. It had been so long since he'd seen her naked. He truly missed her. Missed her laugh, missed her smile, missed her compassion when he was hurt or feeling sad.

But he'd held back. He was sure that he had moved too fast in trying to touch her earlier, and that was what had driven her away. She wouldn't say it out loud to him, but he had replayed it over and over. She ran because he'd pushed her too soon. So, there in the bathroom, he'd refrained. But he couldn't go to bed without knowing she still loved him. This was all for naught if she didn't.

He wouldn't take no for an answer. He couldn't live with that. He pushed the pain from today out of his mind. He saw she had put on the nightshirt that he had bought her, which made him smile.

Tomorrow. Tomorrow will be better.

He replayed the conversation in his mind. He had purposely left out the fact that he *had* seen a doctor about his anger issues, which led to his blackouts, but the guy was a quack. Once, and only once, he had gone to that office. He thought he could handle it all on his own with the relaxation techniques he'd learned that day. He had been wrong. This was more than simply relaxing and working through the anger.

Pushing that thought away, he waited until she was settled in Gram's room and then went around and made sure the doors were still locked. He at least had that piece of mind. She couldn't walk away again without talking to him first. Then he would at least be able to reason with her. They could go home and start over. She'd move back in with him, and the kids would have Mom and Dad back in one home. Kids needed a stable home and two parents together.

Ledge slipped under the covers in his bed and rolled over to face the door. He hoped he'd have a visitor tonight, but he wasn't counting on it. He saw the look of fear on her face when she'd found him in the bathroom. But she *had* told him she loved him, and he could rest easy after hearing that.

No one understood him like Lizabeth did. She was his lifeline.

Something niggled at his brain. He had forgotten something. What was it?

Shit! I have to call Lawson in the morning. Ledge grabbed the alarm clock on the nightstand and set it for 7:30 a.m. Realizing it was almost three in the morning, he made himself comfortable and was soon fast asleep.

Chapter 26

Wednesday

Liza waited until 4:30. Her watch battery had barely 10% left. She'd turned her light off shortly after she'd entered Gram's room. She didn't want Ledge to think she was staying up for any reason.

Which, of course, she was.

She slid out of the room, down the hall, and stopped just before Ledge's bedroom door, which was cracked open. She heard the blessed snoring. A steady, hard snore.

She walked past his room and into the living room, pulling the curtains back at the window. The clouds had cleared, and the moon was making an appearance now. She used that light to see around the room. *Now to find that key.* She knew Ledge was methodical and wouldn't leave the key far from the door, in case there was an emergency. She'd lived with him too long to know he wouldn't risk his own life just to keep her caged.

Looking around the living room, her eyes kept leading her back to the door frame. It would be the perfect hiding place, given her height difference from his. She reached up as high as she could, but she couldn't reach the top of the door frame. She looked around for something to stand on. Nothing. She grabbed a chair from the kitchen and placed it by the front door. Now she could reach the top of the door frame, only to be disappointed. Nothing but dust. She slid over to the nearby picture window and repeated the same step, coming up empty.

She methodically proceeded to check every door frame that she could without making a lot of noise. Only more dust. That left the mudroom door to the outside. Liza moved the chair into position, slid her hand across the top, and again, her fingers found dust …

She heard a clink on the floor.

The key.

She held her breath and listened for other sounds. She wanted to jump up and down and dance crazily in a circle. Instead, she lowered herself from the chair and grabbed the key. She placed it in the dead bolt.

It turned.

Liza stood frozen for a moment, her hand still on the key that was still in the dead bolt. She was torn. She wanted to run right then, but she knew Ledge would wake soon—she'd spent far too much time sneaking around the house with that heavy kitchen chair. Should she go ahead and run, and possibly get caught again? Or should she wait? She couldn't even believe she was debating this with herself.

Reluctantly, she decided to put the key back in its place. At least now she knew where it was. She'd bide her time, and when it happened, hopefully, she would be far away from this prison before he realized she was even gone. And the next time, she wouldn't take the wooded path. She'd learned that lesson.

Liza relocked the dead bolt and replaced the key. She retraced her steps, making sure everything was back in its perfect place. Grabbing a bottle of water from the fridge, she gulped heartily, *thinking, thinking, thinking.* While looking out the window, the barn caught her attention in the moonlight. She walked over to the window and took a good look around at what would normally be the driveway. She didn't see a car. The barn had those old, large, sliding doors on the left side. The attached section had a large door that looked like a taller version of their garage door with a regular walkway door at the far right side. Ledge must have his car in the attached section of the barn, she surmised.

And then another thought came to her. At home, he normally left the keys in the console of the car when it was in the garage. She prayed that his habit hadn't changed. Liza plopped down at the kitchen table. Realization dawned on her that this was the fifth day of her captivity. Her mouth curled into a cry, but she shut it down. She had to stay strong, and she had to get out of this alive. More than anything, the twins needed their mom. And, really, they needed their dad, too. But she couldn't focus on Ledge. She had to focus on her freedom.

Her inner warrior emerged from deep within—a promise to rise in the face of the Demon. To help her maintain that determination, Liza evoked the shock she'd felt the day she found that one text on Ledge's phone …

One night after Ledge had arrived home, he'd left his phone on the dresser instead of taking it into the bathroom with him like he normally did. The phone beeped. Liza was curious and picked it up. There was another woman's name showing. She could still hear Ledge in the shower, singing. She pressed the text to open it. Her hands started to tremble as she read it.

*Tomorrow works great. Can't wait to squeeze that ass!) :-**

Liza choked when she saw the kissy face at the end of the text.

Well, it didn't take a rocket scientist to figure out that was not a text from a client or business partner. Liza was floored. She had suspected he'd been cheating, but reading that text made her suspicions a reality—one that, maybe, she didn't really want to know. She'd deleted the text, and before she could set his phone down, it chimed with an email. She hesitated, but then opened the link. It was to a dating site called marriedmen.com. Another woman had sent a flirty message to him. She almost dropped the phone. He was using a dating site for *married men.*

Liza's stomach churned. She had deleted that email, cleared the trash, and closed the open apps. Then she set his cell phone back on the dresser where she'd found it. She hadn't told anyone. Not even Trinity. That evening had led her to hire a private investigator to ferret out the rest. Sadly, it hadn't taken the PI long to gain the dirty details of Ledge's cheating.

Drawing in a breath, Liza put her emotions in check. She shook off the sick feeling her inner warrior had conjured, driving out the hopelessness she'd felt moments ago. Plotting her escape to freedom, she silently made her way back to Gram's room, taking time to stop and look at Ledge as he slept. Sighing, she allowed herself a little sadness. She missed the good Ledge. The better man he used to be. The one who made her feel alive. Not the one who seemed to want her dead—at least emotionally. And her physical death may not be far behind.

***

Ledge woke with a start. Looking around, he realized it was the alarm going off. It was 7:32—he'd slept through a full two minutes of that alarm. Damn, he'd been tired. He still felt tired. He sat up with a start. Had he woken Lizabeth? He strained his ears but heard nothing. He got up and peeked down the hallway. Her door was still closed.

He headed to the bathroom to start his routine and then make the call to Lawson. He felt certain that Lizabeth would be sleeping for hours still, which gave him the opportunity to call Lawson and reassure him. He hoped. And it would give Ledge time to think about how he could get Lizabeth to loosen up, open up to him. He was running out of time. He could feel it. Phone in hand, he walked to the kitchen to grab a bottle of water before heading out to the barn to make his call.

One bottle was missing. Lizabeth must have been up last night after he went to sleep. He looked around the kitchen and then walked throughout the house. Suspicion pricked at him. But he saw nothing out of the ordinary. Everything was as it should be. He headed toward the back door to keep the noise to a minimum. The front door had a noisy squeak to it when he opened it, and he hadn't WD-40'd the hinges yet. No sense in making his exit known.

He pulled his keys out of his pocket and opened the mudroom door. On a hunch, he shut the door and reached up to feel for the extra key above the door. He knew he could break a window if there was a fire, but having the extra key there for an emergency was his piece of mind. Thankfully, it was still there. *Good.* Breathing a sigh of relief, he walked out and locked the dead bolt behind him.

Off to the barn he went. Turning on the lights in the shop, he prepared himself mentally for the call he needed to make. All was quiet out there. No sounds to alert Lawson—like his mother's voice. Ledge pulled out the bench seat that Gramps had built, dusted it off with his free hand, and sat down. His cell phone dangled from his hand as he looked around the shop. Gramps had hung a countless number of tools on the pegboards. They were covered with rust and dust. He wasn't sure he even remembered what most of them were used for. Glancing at the dreaded object in his hand, he lifted his cell and dialed his son.

Chapter 27

"Hi, Dad!"

"How are you feeling today, son?"

"Better. Lexi and I did get some sleep, which was good. We're at your place. I think being home helps even more, but I know we'd feel better if you were here."

"Well, a few more days, and I'll be there. I wanted to hear your voice and make sure you two were doing okay. I have a meeting shortly. Things are going well on this end. Any word on Mom?"

"No. I haven't heard anything. Aunt Trinity said she'd get in touch with us if she heard anything. All I know is a detective showed up at our dorm to speak to us yesterday. We freaked out, and that's why I called you."

Ledge felt his skin prickle. "What did he ask you?"

"I was the last one who called Mom before she disappeared. He wanted to see if there was anything about the call that might lead us to her. I don't feel like I was much help."

"That's okay. Don't put pressure on yourself. This is not your fault. She's probably enjoying her vacation, maybe took a detour. Oh, I'm being motioned to go into the meeting. They're ready for me. I don't know how reachable I'll be today, so text me. I'll try to look at my phone again later tonight. Love you."

"Love you, too, Dad."

***

Lawson had a puzzled looked on his face. "That was weird."

"What?" Lexi asked.

"Dad didn't ask much about Mom being missing. Like it was no big deal, nothing to worry about. It's been, like, five days, Lexi! Then he said he had to go into a meeting. I thought he'd at least ask what everyone was doing to find her. And more logically, drop what he was doing and come home. I know he still loves her. So, why isn't he more worried?"

"He's probably focused on gaining new clients. And he's probably not trying to worry us any more than we already are. He always downplays bad situations. We need to do what we can do, and that is to keep studying. Mom wouldn't want us worrying about her. You know how proud she was when we both made the Dean's List last year."

"You're probably right. He said he'd check back this evening. Hopefully by then, we'll have more information. This 'not knowing' is killing me."

"Me too, Laws. Me too." Lexi patted her brother's shoulder and leaned in for a hug.

They headed to the kitchen, where they had dropped their backpacks. Silently, they pulled out their books and tried to study. After a few moments, their eyes met, and they shook their heads in unison. They knew they needed to study, but it wasn't going to happen this morning. They were too worried. Too confused.

Lexi said, "Let's get out of here."

Lawson gave her a small smile. "Works for me. Let's grab some muffins and hot cappuccinos, and then go see Aunt Trinity. I think I remember she said she was taking today off … and maybe tomorrow, too."

"Sounds great. We can get homework done later this afternoon." Grinning at her brother, she grabbed her purse and keys from the kitchen counter, and they hit the road.

***

Ledge sat there with his cell in his hand. He hated lying to his children, but if he was going to make his family whole again, it was a necessary evil. His mind wandered back to earlier that spring, shortly after he had been caught with that *tramp*. That tramp had cost him dearly. His Life. His World. His Lizabeth, who had left him cold and empty, as if he had never held her, never loved her.

He recalled that day vividly, the day he truly realized Lizabeth wasn't kidding around. The day his emotions hit him hard, the day the divorce papers had been handed to him as he approached his car. Thankfully, he had been alone, leaving work. No coworkers had been with him when the stranger smiled and held out the large envelope. No words were spoken; the man walked away, leaving Ledge scratching his head, wondering what the hell had just happened. His curiosity got the best of him, and he opened the envelope. He laughed when he read the court papers and tossed them into the passenger seat, denying they existed, then he started the car and pulled out onto Wackerly Street.

Ledge headed home and was surprised to find the radio tuned to '80s music on the satellite radio—not something he typically listened to. Then he realized it was his daughter's doing. Alexis was interning at his office and had used his car earlier that day to deliver proofs to a client.

He didn't change the station and, instead, allowed himself to be immersed in the bass of the current song. Alexis had always loved listening to his and Lizbeth's old records, and the thought made him smile. He tapped his hand on the steering wheel, even bobbed his head a little. As he pulled into his driveway, another song came on—one that he'd never much paid attention to, the lyrics and all. But that time, he did, and he had been struck with the deep meaning of the song. A song that now infested his soul with every single word: "Against all Odds" by Phil Collins.

He remembered feeling the pain in the words, in himself. He had pulled into the garage, closed the garage door, but he didn't move from the car. He was lost in his misery. His grip on the steering wheel tightened, and tears began to fall down his cheeks.

His foot fell heavy on the gas pedal—engine revving. It wasn't until the fumes hit him and he began to cough uncontrollably that he realized what was happening.

Frantically, he swiped at the garage-door remote and turned off the car.

He remembered how his chest had been pounding, like never before in his life. How he struggled to breathe—for so many reasons. How he'd hefted himself out of the car and rushed out onto the driveway, sucking in the fresh air.

Even as he calmed himself, he knew his mind was taking him to dark places more and more frequently. He knew he needed to talk to someone.

And he had. He'd called his best friend Ollie ...

Had he subconsciously wanted to take his own life back then?

Perhaps, although he didn't really think so. He had never been one to throw in the towel when there were options. And there were always options.

Chapter 28

Trinity was on the phone with Chrissie when her phone dinged, a text from Lawson asking her what kind of coffee and muffin she wanted. She put her call on speaker and texted him back.

Trinity: *I don't need anything. I have had too much coffee already. Thanks.* ☺

Lawson: *Are you sure? We're heading to your house, and we're standing in line right now.*

Trinity: *I'm good. Drive safe!*

She left her phone on speaker and set it down to finish listening to Chrissie and her barrage of questions. Finally able to get a word in, she said, "No, I haven't heard anything yet, but I'm going to call if I don't hear from them this morning. I'm sure they're tired of the many calls I made to them yesterday, checking in."

"As soon as you find out *anything,* let me know. I'm like a walking dead person over here. Kyle and his friends have been great about trying to keep my mind off of it, but once I get back to my cabin, all the what-ifs take over, and I'm a mess again. I realize worrying here or at home doesn't make any difference, but I'm close enough to the edge that I am ready to wait it out at home with you."

"I get it, but if you come home now, you'd be pacing here like me. Stay on board. At least you can have plenty to keep you occupied. We don't need two of us running around town like crazy people. I'd call the department right now, but the twins are on their way over, and I don't want to be in the middle of all that when they get here."

"The twins! Oh my God! I haven't even thought about how they're handling all of this. Are they okay?"

"They're okay. Lawson took it pretty hard that he was the last person to talk to her. Lexi had texted me last night to let me know they'd made it to their dad's house. She drove because Lawson was such a mess, beating himself up that he hadn't been much help to Detective Hannah."

"Oh. That's not his fault. Nothing he could do."

"That's what I told him. And I'll remind him again when they get here."

"Good. Well, since the kids are on their way and I'm an exhausted pile of crap right now, I'm going to take a sleeping pill and, hopefully, get some rest. I haven't slept very much, and last night's show really hurt to finish."

"Get your sleep. As usual, anything I hear, you'll be the first person I call. Love ya!"

"Thanks, Trin! Sorry I'm not home to hang with you during all of this."

"Like I said, it's for the best. Plus, Ollie has been tremendous."

"Good old Ollie. I'm glad he's there for you. Okay, bye. Love ya."

And Chrissie was gone. Trinity blew out a breath. She was exhausted herself. She'd barely slept last night. She had come out to the living room to watch some TV so she didn't keep Ollie awake with her tossing and turning. The hours had seemed like days until she had finally given up and started her day.

Soon, the twins were knocking at the front door. When she opened it, they swooped in, set their coffee and muffins on the foyer table, and gave her a bear hug. They stood there like that for a long time, the three of them, until finally breaking apart and wiping a few tears from their eyes.

"So, how are you two holding up?" Trinity asked as she led them to the living room.

"We're doing better today. I think it helped staying at home instead of the dorms, even if Dad wasn't there," Lawson said. Lexi nodded. They both sat and sipped on their cappuccinos.

"So, your dad's not home?" Trinity's curiosity was piqued.

Lawson said, "He's on a business trip. I think he said he was in Chicago, or ... wait, he didn't say. I remember he wanted to go to Chicago to expand his customer base." He frowned. "Kinda weird. Usually, he lets us know where he is."

"What's wrong, Laws?" Lexi asked.

"It's odd, isn't it? That dad didn't tell us where he was going before he left? He always lets us know."

She shrugged it off. "Maybe a little strange, but he probably knew how swamped we'd be with college and didn't think it was necessary. Even with the divorce, he always checks in with us eventually. He's dealing with a bunch of things, I'm sure."

"I guess. I just …We used to be closer, is all. This past summer, things were … different."

Meanwhile, Trinity's wheels were spinning. It wasn't like Ledge to pull away from his kids and not let them know when he was going out of town and to where. Both those kids were his world. He doted on them like Liza did. Something wasn't right.

"So, when is the last time you talked to your dad?" Trinity tried to maintain a poker face as she prayed that Ledge wasn't involved in her friend's disappearance. His anger issues, his fidelity issues, the divorce that he didn't want …

She couldn't shake the chill that snaked down her spine. She couldn't shake her growing suspicion about Ledge.

But she plastered on a smile for her honorary niece and nephew, reassuring them and then catching up on their lives.

On the inside, she vowed to visit that police station once the twins had left and demand to have a talk with that detective. No more pussy-footing around.

***

Lawson's gears were turning, he listened as Aunt Trinity and Lexi talked small talk. He knew what she was up to—anything to help take their minds off the bloated elephant in the room. His mind wandered back to the earlier conversation he'd had with his dad this week after telling him Mom was missing. It was all on repeat in his mind: Dad's lack of concern, his dismissive responses, and his self-absorbed attitude about his business.

Lexi's voice wandered into his reminiscence.

"No, I think Dad misses Mom more than he lets on. I can't believe he is so blasé about it all. It's not like him to not be concerned, even if they are divorced. There are still ties, ya know? Especially about something as serious as Mom missing."

Laws watched Lexi twist her fingers in her sweatshirt—she had just thrown on whatever her eyes first saw when she woke up. He had done the same—pulling jeans off the floor, ones that had a stain on them from last night's quick supper. He absentmindedly picked it as he listened to his sister's words. She was trying to be the strong one, but he knew she was a wreck, just like he was a wreck.

Trinity said, "I'm sure your Dad has a lot on his mind, but—" she wagged her finger in the air "—I have to admit it bothers me, too, that he hasn't immediately come home to help with the search or anything."

Trinity almost snarled the last part, but Laws saw her catch herself midsentence. He could tell that Lexi had noticed it, too, but he chose not to say anything about it. He felt as if he were watching them all on TV. He felt removed somehow, seeing things for what they were. Then a wild thought slapped him in the head. He sat and chewed on his lower lip, allowing the thought to take purchase. He knew what he—what they— needed to do when they got home, and suddenly, he wanted to leave so they could get started. If they could find even the smallest of a clue at home, it might help the detectives find their mother.

Lawson lamented on that last thought. What if that clue led them to their dad as the perpetrator? Had Dad killed their mother? Or was she still alive? Or was Lawson just worrying about nothing?

Lawson shuddered as a cold sensation took over his body. If there was a chance their mother was still alive, they would find that clue; they would find her. Even if that meant Dad was responsible, a criminal, a wolf in sheep's clothing. Lawson couldn't fathom it, but reality wasn't always a warm blanket.

He pushed himself off the couch, and both Trinity and Lexi looked his way with curiosity.

"Sorry. I hate to interrupt, but I think we should get going, Lexi. We have to finish our homework, and I'm getting hungry. Want to stop at Bob's for a quick bite?"

Lexi agreed, and they said their goodbyes. Trinity's hug was reassuring, and he was glad they had come. Now it was time to step off the sidelines and onto the field.

Time to find their mom.

Chapter 29

Trinity rushed to answer the call.

"Mrs. Gold? This is Detective Hannah. You stopped by to see me earlier?"

"Yes. Is there any news on Liza McAllister?"

"We're working the case. I spoke with Lawson yesterday, as you probably know. We're also working with the sheriff's department to check MBS airport, since that's their jurisdiction. That's all I have for you at this time."

"So, basically, still no lead on Liza." Feeling deflated again, Trinity released a heavy sigh.

"Sorry, ma'am. We've pooled our resources and will follow each lead as they come in. If you have any other information about this case, please let me know as soon as possible."

She thought about mentioning Ledge, her suspicions. But was it her place to cast shadow on a person when she had no real proof? In the end, she decided to keep it to herself, at least until she knew for sure—if she would ever know for sure. "Thank you, Detective. We're hopeful this will end well. I'll stay in touch, as I'm sure you're well aware of by now."

The detective chuckled at that. "Yes, ma'am. We appreciate you checking in. I'm sorry I'm not always available to take your call."

"I understand. I realize it's because you're doing your job."

She disconnected and felt her frustration mount. Dead ends everywhere, it seemed.

A trip to the gym might ease her mind and body. She was exhausted mentally, but not physically—and in order to sleep well, a tired body was the ticket. She sent a quick Facebook message to Chrissie to let her know nothing else had turned up. Once again, she said nothing about her Ledge suspicions. She was probably just grasping at straws there, anyway. The detectives would certainly handle it if they felt there was reason to pursue him.

Right? At least she had watched enough ID Channel to know they couldn't arrest anyone with only a "suspicion."

She called work and let them know she was going to use two more vacation days. Payroll wasn't until next week, and she prayed Liza was found by then—safe and intact. She grabbed her gym bag and headed out, determined to work her every muscle to the hilt.

***

Detective Hannah mulled over the lack of evidence for the case. He had stayed late at the office, into the early morning hours. He wanted to wait until the crime lab had finished their work, just in case they found something he could use. Nothing had turned up.

The kids knew nothing. Ms. McAllister's best friends knew little to nothing. Her coworkers knew nothing. In fact, Ann, the receptionist, had broken into tears when he'd told her the news, why he was there asking questions. Her boss, the staff … no one could come up with any client that she or the firm had worked with that would have cause to be disgruntled with Ms. McAllister. He'd left them his card and walked out, hoping someone—anyone—would remember a detail, no matter how small, and it would help him break this frustrating case.

So far, he knew these facts:

- Ms. McAllister had a heart of gold.

- Ms. McAllister was a great person to have around.

- Ms. McAllister was a great mom.

- Ms. McAllister was a great friend.

"Big buncha nothing," he muttered to himself.

Hannah scratched his chin and swiveled in his chair.

What does the ex-husband, Ledge McAllister, know?

Hannah understood they were recently divorced and that Ledge had not contested it, even if he wasn't thoroughly on board with it. The two hadn't spoken in months, based on his inquiries with people in her circle.

But maybe they had.

But the guy was out of town on business when all this happened. Hannah had learned that tidbit from the firm when he'd called to speak with Mr. McAllister. They told him he would not be back until Monday. Days from now. Hannah hadn't left a message. If Ledge McAllister was working elsewhere when his ex-wife went missing, then it couldn't have been him.

Right?

They had his cell number. Though Hannah would prefer a face-to-face with Ledge, he knew it was time to make the call, given the lack of progress.

First, he would join Reyes for their scheduled lunch to discuss the case.

Second, they would have another chat with the twins. The kids may know more than they thought they did.

Third, he would call Ledge McAllister.

Check that: first, he would make a call to the sheriff's office and see what they'd found out regarding Ms. McAllister's flight information. Lunch would have to wait a few more minutes. His stomach growled with discontent.

***

Sheriff Sarah Crawford was about to dial the phone at the Saginaw County Sheriff's Office when it rang, causing her to jump. She took a breath and answered, "Sheriff Crawford."

"Good afternoon. This Detective Sergeant Hannah. I'm checking back in to see how things turned out regarding the flight information for Ms. McAllister."

"I was actually dialing your number. I wanted to give you an update before shift change. I can tell you Ms. McAllister *did* have a flight booked out of MBS early Saturday morning, arriving in Detroit to catch a flight out of there to San Juan, arriving later that evening in San Juan. She *did not* board that flight to Detroit. I had them check other flight records to see if she boarded any other flight on any other airline." Nothing."

Crawford put her phone on speaker in her closed office so she could pull her long, light-brown hair back into a bun. Her gray eyes searched her notes while she tamed her hair. She may not have had the size and muscle of her male colleagues, but she took her position seriously.

She continued. "So ... on a hunch, I checked the parking lot. After driving through a few sections, I found Ms. McAllister's white Chevy pickup truck. The license plate matched the BOLO. I radioed Deputy Erickson at MBS, to keep a close eye on the vehicle and inform me if it left the airport. I went back to the terminal to pull the surveillance tapes from Friday until today. It'll take some time to finish going through those, but I have a deputy reviewing the tapes now. No one at the airport recognized her from the driver's license photo you emailed me. I also checked into all rental-car businesses located at MBS, and they did not have a rental car listed under Ms. McAllister's name, and no one at any of those locations recognized her picture, either."

"Sheriff Crawford, I appreciate your assistance. And persistence. I'm anxious to hear what transpires with your findings today. Keep me in the loop."

"Not a problem. Will do."

"Until then."

"Until then."

Hannah hung up and immediately started the process of a search warrant to retrieve Ms. McAllister's truck from the MBS parking lot. After handing the paperwork to Reyes to get it signed, he sat back, tapped his pen on his desk, and reviewed the scribbled notes he had taken. *So, you went to the airport, but no one has seen you. The tapes should be interesting if they can tell us who was driving the vehicle. Very interesting.*

Sure, Ms. McAllister *could* have run off with a friend, but the blood on the floor and the broken glass in an otherwise spotless house portrayed a more sinister picture. And with her cell phone found under the couch, he was certain she'd been abducted. But CSI had found nothing but smudged prints or prints that had been ruled out, and no other evidence to explain her sudden disappearance.

What's your story, Ms. McAllister?

Hannah felt strongly that the ex-husband was involved. And his hunches were normally spot-on, or close to it. He needed a solid piece of evidence to get a search warrant for Mr. McAllister's house and for his phone records. He couldn't ping his location without it.

He let his mind continue to wander through theories as he headed out to meet Reyes.

Mr. McAllister had a hot temper, according to Mrs. Gold, and his business trip just happened to be the same week that his ex-wife was supposed to be taking a cruise, but … *surprise*, she didn't make the cruise.

Hannah didn't believe in coincidences.

Chapter 30

"So, you cool with my plan?" Lawson asked between bites of his juicy burger. They'd stopped at Bob's and were now sitting at the kitchen table in their home, stuffing their faces in between discussing Lawson's idea.

"Yes. I'm still not sure we should, but I'm not buying Dad's act, either. The more I think about it, the less it makes sense." She hesitated then asked, "Laws...what if we find something? What if—" Lexi halted her words, and her face paled.

"Don't think about that now. We have to stay strong for Mom. We don't know Dad is involved, but he's definitely not acting like I would expect at the news that Mom's missing. I know they're divorced and all, but Dad would still be concerned, even pissed and ready to tear someone apart. I pray he's not involved, but things aren't adding up." Laws tossed his burger down on the wrapper. "I'm not hungry anymore. You ready?"

"Let's do this. The sooner we search the house, the sooner we'll know," Lexi said as she stood.

"Okay, I think we should start in Dad's office. Do you want that room or the bedroom?" Lawson looked back at Lexi as he headed upstairs.

"I'll take the office. Since Mom's not here anymore, it's probably better that you search the bedroom."

"On it." Lawson took the steps two at a time as he headed for the bedroom.

Neither of them wanted to find anything ... incriminating. And they didn't want their dad to know they'd searched through his belongings. So they searched with caution and care.

Lawson stopped suddenly when his eyes landed on a safe in the closet. "Lexi! Come here!"

"What is it?" she asked as she bolted into the room.

"Not sure it's anything, really. There's a small safe here." He pointed. "Have you seen any keys lying around? We need to know what's in there."

"No, not that I've seen. Dad might have them on his key ring, for all I know."

"Probably. Maybe. We should keep looking."

"Right. I'll keep my eyes peeled." Lexi wandered back to the office.

***

Detective Hannah had just received the results of the inspection of Ms. McAllister's truck. The effort had netted them a pretty penny. Her packed luggage was found in the bed under a locked tonneau cover. The clothes revealed she had, in fact, packed for a cruise. There were a few bathing suits, shorts, tank tops, flip-flops, sandals, summer dresses, and evening clothes. But that wasn't all they found. The seat was positioned far back from the steering wheel—way too far for a woman who was only five feet five inches tall.

Earlier that afternoon, Crawford had called and shared with him that the surveillance tapes revealed Ms. McAllister *had not* entered the airport. Now, after finding this tasty tidbit on the driver's seat, Hannah picked up his phone and dialed Crawford.

"Well, that was an interesting find," Crawford said as she sat up straighter in her chair, alert to the new evidence.

"Agreed," Hannah replied. "Could you revisit the videotapes again and look for Mr. McAllister? I believe you should keep the focus on early-morning Saturday. One of the neighbors said they were up at the time and saw a car pull into Ms. McAllister's residence. I'm willing to bet it was him."

"For sure. I'll get my guys on it straightaway. Do you have a recent photo of him?"

"I think the easiest way is if you look up the picture of Mr. McAllister on his business website: McAllister Designs. It's a better picture than we could pull from the driver's license, which is three years old."

"Doing that now. I'll get back to you as soon as we know. Until then." And Crawford hung up.

Hannah had a feeling Crawford would find Ledge McAllister on the surveillance videos. They had lifted prints from the truck, but nothing had come up in AFIS – the Automated Fingerprint Identification System. That only meant that the person of interest was not in the system. Yet.

Chapter 31

After the light went out in Gram's room, indicating Lizabeth had settled in for the night, Ledge walked around and checked all the doors—twice. He was tired, so very tired, but his body wouldn't let him sleep. He took out a deck of cards and sat at the kitchen table.

She had been agreeable this afternoon. Suspiciously pleasant and quite flirty. Or maybe she was coming around. He'd let her sleep most of the day. He hadn't wanted to rock the boat, especially as he felt the urgency of the situation weigh heavy on his shoulders. Then he remembered. *Shit!* He was supposed to have called Lawson.

He went to his room and locked the door. He didn't want to chance going out to the barn, since Liza had only recently put out her light. He took his phone off the charger and turned it on. It started to beep with "missed call and text" notices. He quickly silenced it and clicked on missed calls.

There were several missed calls. Two from a number he didn't know, and one from Lawson, two from Ollie, as well as one text from Ollie. He quickly viewed the text.

Hey man, Liza is missing and you're not answering your phone. Give me a call. We're all concerned. Later.

He didn't bother listening to Ollie's voice message. He wouldn't call Ollie, anyway, because that man was just too intuitive. He'd know right away that something was off. No way Ledge could chance that.

He dialed Lawson and hoped he was still awake—it was already 10:30 p.m.

"Hey, Dad," a yawning Lawson answered after the third ring.

"Hey, buddy. How was your day? Any news about Mom?" He was trying to sound concerned and to keep his voice low at the same time.

"No, nothing today. I called Aunt Trinity before I called you. Still nothing from the cops or anyone. She was going to check in again with the police tomorrow. How was your day? Any good contracts?"

"Yes, actually, it was very productive. I think things are moving well, and I should be able to come home early."

"That's great! Lexi and I could really use you home right now. When do you think you'll be home?"

"Maybe by Friday morning. I'll need to check the flight schedule. Of course, I need to wrap things up here tomorrow."

"That's great. Maybe even catch a flight back tomorrow night? I hope we have news about Mom by then. This is really worrying us, Dad. She never leaves without telling us where she is, and it's not like her to go this long without being in touch with either of us. I know we live a few minutes away, but she always calls to ask how things are going after a few days." Chuckling, he added, "At least she stopped texting us every day after the first month we were at college."

Ledge laughed, too. "You know she missed you guys. You're still her babies."

"I know, Dad. Hey, thanks for calling back. I know you're busy, but it's good to hear your voice with all this going on. It's hard to study. But I think it'd be worse if we were still at the college and trying to handle all this."

"No problem, buddy. Sorry that I've been away when you need me."

"No worries. We're making do. Love ya."

"Love you, too."

Lawson ended the call. Ledge felt good about the conversation. The kids were still concerned for their mother, but Lawson hadn't pressed him about the situation other than wanting him to come home. Ledge felt certain that they didn't suspect him of any wrongdoing. *Why would they, anyway? I'm their dad!*

Ledge took a quick peek into the hallway to make sure Lizabeth's door was still closed. It was, so he locked his bedroom door again and pulled up the voicemail from the unknown number. He had a bad feeling about it—unknown numbers were never anything good.

"Mr. McAllister, this is Detective Sergeant Hannah from the Midland Police Department. I'm sure you've heard by now that I'm investigating the disappearance of your ex-wife, Ms. McAllister." Ledge recoiled when he heard him call Lizabeth his *ex-wife.* "I would like to ask you a few questions, see if you could help the investigation along. I've been informed you're out of town, so if you could call the department at your earliest convenience, I would appreciate it." He rattled off the number where he could be reached, left his name again, and hung up.

Fuck me!

Ledge immediately turned off his phone. That would be the last thing he needed—for them to trace his call when he called back. He needed to think. He was starting to panic. He was so close to reconciling with Lizabeth. He could feel it. He needed only one more day. If they figured out he wasn't on a business trip, they'd definitely try to pin a crime on him.

The panic built inside him. Anger. Frustration. Ledge walked out of his bedroom and headed to the mudroom to leave the house.

Hesitating in the doorway, tapping his finger on the outside doorknob, he reached up to check for the spare key. *Still there.* Ledge clutched his fingers around it like a worry stone, looked at it, and put it in his pocket. He locked up the house and jogged to the barn. Inside the shop, he turned on the light and started pacing. "This is not good. Not good at all. Now, what do I do to stall the detective?"

Pacing like a caged inmate awaiting the death sentence, Ledge decided to move to the interior of the barn. He needed more air than the shop held, and he didn't want to be pacing outside in the moonlight. He walked to the back of the barn and came to a stop at the stairs that led to the old hayloft turned storage area. He stared up at the shadowy space.

His heart started beating even faster than it already was.

He climbed the stairs to the loft, and the memories (and musty smells) hit him hard. All the clothes, toys, and Christmas decorations ... stuffed away.

He let his hand glide over the dusty items and torn boxes, missing his brother John, missing his family. As he headed back to the stairs, something caught his attention in one of the boxes. He walked over to the box and pulled it up, so it stood on its end. Inside was the punching bag that used to hang downstairs. A flash memory came to him: he saw himself sitting on a bale of hay, watching John punching that bag and Gramps coaching John.

He remembered he didn't get to take a turn because he wasn't quite tall enough to reach it. John was four years older, taller, and stronger.

Well, now Ledge was taller and stronger. He pulled the big punching bag all the way out and tossed it over his shoulder. He carried it downstairs, listening to the rusty chains jangling as he bounced down the stairs. The hook where the bag used to hang was still there, on a beam under the loft. He placed the punching bag into position, rolled up his sleeves, and started punching. The feel of the bag was cold against his fists. He let the hurt and anger fly free with every punch he threw.

***

Liza heard murmuring coming from Ledge's room. She silently opened Gram's bedroom door and looked into the hall. His door was closed. She tiptoed out of the room, making her way toward the closed door. She'd go into the bathroom as a backup plan if he exited before she had a chance to listen in. Making her way as stealthily as she could, she arrived at Ledge's bedroom without interference, took a deep breath, and listened. Ledge was talking to someone. *Who? And why the hell can't I get a signal but he can?* Liza looked down at her watch, texted another message to Trinity, and sent it.

The connection failed, as the tiny lit screen clearly indicated. She'd been trying off and on from different rooms earlier in the day when Ledge wasn't looking, but nothing was getting out. *This watch is useless!*

And then the screen went black. Liza nearly blacked out, too. She hit the screen, the power button … nothing. The battery had finally died. Staring at the expensive waste of money on her wrist, she vaguely realized that Ledge had stopped talking. Panicked, Liza almost tripped over her feet as she stepped back from the door and backtracked down the hall. Safely in her room, she slipped into bed and tried to calm her thumping heart.

She heard Ledge yank his door open and trudge toward the kitchen. His ominous footfalls made her body flinch with every step he made … until she could no longer hear them. Liza slowly let out the air she'd been holding trying to listen. She waited. And waited.

Liza heard nothing more, which was strange. She fully expected to hear some movement or sound from somewhere in the house. Maybe he had returned to his room, and she hadn't heard him. She uncurled her cramped fingers from the covers she hadn't realized she'd been gripping in fear. Although her breathing had slowed, her mind was whirling with questions. *Who was he talking to? Why was he chancing using his cell phone? They have to be searching for me, right?* She needed to move, evaluate the situation. She'd feign needing a drink of water if she ran into Ledge.

Liza crept from the bed, trying to stay calm as she manufactured nonchalance exiting the bedroom. She stopped in her tracks in the hallway. The house was silent. She maintained her faux confidence and walked toward the kitchen, glancing in each room, watching for any movement. Her ears were on high alert, listening for any sound. All was quiet and empty as she reached the dark kitchen. She saw a flash of movement on her right. She whipped around to defend herself. Nothing. *What the hell?*

Liza pulled her arms down and slowly moved toward the kitchen window, trying to seek out the creator of the object that had spooked her. There at the garage was a figure standing at the walkway door. *Ledge.* Her shoulders dropped, momentarily releasing the tension she was carrying. She watched him walk in and flip on the light. She grabbed a bottle of water from the fridge and watched out the window. The clock was ticking on the wall. Her body was edgy and wanted to run, but she wasn't sure how long he was going to be out there.

No, she'd bide her time and wait for him to come back inside and go to bed. Sparring with herself, Liza's inner warrior won out—stick to the plan. Act, don't react. She walked back down the hall with her bottle of water, climbed in bed, and waited for the sound of his return.

Chapter 32

Thursday

Sheriff Crawford had called late last night. She believed she found a man who resembled McAllister, even though he'd been wearing a hat. He had gotten into a cab after walking to the entrance of the airport from the MBS parking lot. Ms. McAllister's truck was parked in a spot where they couldn't see who had exited the truck. But the timeline fit for when her truck had entered the airport parking lot and when the man appeared, walking toward the airport doors. The man had then waited for the cab out front of the airport entrance. He had no bags with him.

After receiving the call from Crawford, Hannah had called the taxi service she'd mentioned. The taxi company had closed for the evening. He had to wait to speak with them when they reopened after six this morning. He was currently en route now to interview the taxi company owner to see who had placed a call for pick-up around the time that Crawford had given him. Maybe he could even speak to the driver of the cab.

Meanwhile, he was hoping for a return call from Mr. McAllister and had the department on alert to trace the call when it came in. He needed the cab driver's verification to seal the deal—that it was indeed Mr. McAllister who had been his passenger. Hannah arrived at the taxi company and walked in.

Detective Hannah was greeted by the dispatcher, who informed him the owner was not present, but he would be willing to help find the information the detective sought. After searching for only a minute, the dispatcher found the reservation for the Saturday-morning MBS pickup, set for 5:30 a.m. It was for a Gerald Hamp, to be dropped off at The H, a well-known hotel in Midland. The driver who had picked up Mr. Hamp was about to come on duty. The dispatcher handed Hannah the phone number on record from the taxi request.

While Detective Sergeant Hannah waited for the driver, he thought about the drop-off location. Then he realized it was only six blocks away from Ms. McAllister's home. He planned to stop at The H after he was done with the driver. He'd see if anyone recognized Mr. McAllister.

Right then, the driver walked over and introduced himself.

"Hello, Detective. I'm Justin Clark."

Shaking his hand, Hannah wasted no time and pulled Mr. McAllister's picture from his pocket.

"Did you pick up this man on Saturday morning from the airport?"

Justin squinted at the picture for a few seconds, and then he nodded. "Yeah. Yep, I remember that guy. I think his name was Mr. Hamp. Picked him up at 5:30."

"Did Mr. Hamp have any luggage?"

"No, I asked him about that, and he said the airport had lost it."

"I see, and where did you drop Mr. Hamp off?"

"The H Hotel."

"Did Mr. Hamp say anything during the drive?"

"No, he was very quiet during the trip, but he did give me a big tip."

"Did Mr. Hamp pay for the ride with a credit card?"

"No, he paid in cash, which I don't like to take, but he said that's all he had on him. I found that odd, but I had to accept it or lose the fair."

"I see. And you're sure Mr. Hamp was this man in the picture?"

"Yes, he was wearing a ball cap, though, and glasses."

"Thank you for your time, Justin."

Detective Hannah walked out of the building, feeling satisfied. He had verification that it was Mr. McAllister at the airport. Now he could get the warrant to search Mr. McAllister's premises. Finally, some progress. And he was looking forward to more.

He called HQ to see if Mr. McAllister had called in, which he hadn't, and then he asked for Detective Reyes. Hannah relayed all the information he recently acquired and asked his partner to get the warrant started. He told Reyes he was on his way to The H to see what else he could find out. He'd be back at HQ within the hour. He highly doubted Mr. McAllister had actually gone into the hotel, but he needed to cross all the t's and dot all the i's.

When the clerk at the desk, who had been working the Saturday morning shift, denied ever having checked in, or seen, the man in the picture, Hannah knew he had dotted another i.

Hannah didn't bother asking for security camera tapes, because he already knew where Mr. McAllister had gone after being dropped at the hotel. A passenger from the airport would not appear suspicious if dropped at a hotel. And the suspect would certainly not want to be delivered to the crime scene.

Hannah headed back to his car and thought through the whole scenario. He figured the suspect had driven himself to Ms. McAllister's place, and over powered her. Detained her in some way, and drove her truck to the airport for appearances. Then he got his cab ride back here to the hotel, and walked back to her house. It was only a few blocks from here. They had not found a garage door remote in Ms. McAllister's truck, even though they had noticed the indentation where an opener would have been—on the visor above the driver's seat. The suspect must have used the remote to regain access into Ms. McAllister's home.

Hannah drove the few short blocks to Ms. McAllister's. He circled her block and then retraced his path back to The H. His objective was to find any locations along the way that may have video surveillance that he could use to his benefit. He knew what McAllister drove, but he may have rented a car, not wanting to be seen in his own vehicle.

***

Lawson and Lexi had netted nothing searching all the rooms in the house last night. Exhaustion had overtaken them before they even got to the garage. They had methodically searched all the drawers, cupboards, and any hidey-holes they could see. No key was found to open the safe, either.

The next morning, Lawson wasted no time in heading toward the garage to continue that part of the search. He'd left his sister upstairs to sleep.

But she wasn't asleep. "Laws, do you want to grab something from town for breakfast this morning?" she hollered. She was in the kitchen area, he guessed, looking for him.

Lawson frowned after putting the last container on the shelf in the garage. Nothing. He turned toward the kitchen to respond to his sister, and in doing so, knocked his father's jacket off the hook on the wall. When he picked it up and brushed the dust off, a piece of paper fell from the pocket onto the floor. Puzzled, he picked up the small, folded piece of paper and brought it with him into the kitchen.

"Oh, there you are. I was asking ..." Lexi stopped when she saw her brother holding up the folded paper. She pointed at it. "What'd you find?"

He shrugged, unfolded the paper, read it. He gasped, throwing his right hand over his mouth when he read the two words scribbled in his dad's handwriting:

Cruise October

Lawson couldn't speak, so he turned the paper toward his sister so she could read it, too.

Her reaction was the same as his.

When had their dad found out about their mom's vacation plans? Why had he made note of it? Why?

Tears welled in Lexi's eyes as she looked at her brother.

He wished he could make her tears go away, but he was having a hard enough time dealing with his own.

Chapter 33

After relentlessly searching for an external video camera in the connecting paths to Liza McAllister's home, Hannah came up empty and frustrated. As he pulled up to turn into Ms. McAllister's driveway, he was astonished to see another vehicle already there.

Interesting. The crime-scene tape was still over the doors, and the property hadn't been released yet.

Hannah then saw an older man walking toward the vehicle and talking on the phone, a puzzled look on his face.

Hannah hopped out of his unmarked police car and flashed his badge.

The man disconnected his call and visibly relaxed. "Can you tell me what's going on?" The man gestured at the tape surrounding the area.

"I'm Detective Sergeant Hannah, and you are?"

"The property owner. What's going on? Is Ms. McAllister ... dead?" He paled when he said the last word.

"We're investigating her disappearance. There was a disturbance in the home; we believe she was taken against her will."

Sometimes the blunt "wow" factor was what the detective used to check people's responses. This guy was not faking his emotions.

"Oh, shit! Shit ... sorry, Detective."

"No problem. Can I get your name?

"Lawrence Carpenter. I rent this home to Liza."

"What brings you here today?"

"She asked me to check the plumbing in the bathroom while she was gone. I guess the drain is backing up in the shower. I tried calling her right now, but it went to voicemail. And then ... you."

"I see. Do you happen to know Ms. McAllister very well?"

"Yes, she's a dear friend of Trinity and Oliver Gold. She's such a sweet girl. A shame what her ex did to her, cheating on her and all."

"Yes, so ... about Mr. McAllister. Have you seen him around here at all?"

"I wouldn't know, but after what Trinity told me about the cheating and that Liza was looking for a secluded location to stay, I suggested this house. It's not easily seen from the street, and it has a garage. The back yard is also secluded. I gave her a key the day she saw it, and she moved in shortly after."

"Do you know if she kept a spare key hidden outside anywhere?" There had been no sign of a break-in, and the front door had been locked when the Golds arrived to check on their friend days ago. Would Liza have opened her door to her abductor? To Ledge McAllister?

"Not that I'm aware of. I do know that she didn't want Mr. McAllister to bother her, and she figured having a secluded home was a way for her to feel safe. Or at least not be easily seen. She wanted her privacy."

"Did you happen to come here before Ms. McAllister left for vacation?"

"No. She said it was okay to check while she was gone. That way, if there was a repair that needed to be done, she wouldn't be in the middle of it."

"Thank you for your time, Mr. Carpenter. Here's my card, in case you think of anything else."

"I am probably not going to be much help. The house was recently remodeled, and the drain was the only complaint she'd had. She's been an on-time paying tenant, and she makes a mean chocolate Bundt cake. That's all I know. I haven't needed to come over here for anything prior to today."

"Thank you. I appreciate your time."

"I'll keep her in my prayers. This is so surreal."

"That it is. Also, this case is still under investigation, so please refrain from entering the house."

"I won't go in, Detective. I didn't, as you can see."

"Appreciate it."

They both headed to their vehicles. Just as Hannah closed his door, his phone went off. It was Reyes.

"You got it?" Hannah asked without any greeting. "We got it. We got the warrant," Reyes said.

"What's the address again?" Reyes told him, and Hannah said, "Meet me there."

The detective pulled out of the driveway, squealing the wheels a bit in the process. He flipped a goodbye wave to Mr. Carpenter, who was still standing next to his car, looking dazed.

Hannah would have a look at the house later. He wanted to see if anyone had returned.

Heading down the road, he allowed himself a small smile. He was feeling that buzz of energy when he was hot on a trail.

Then his smile washed away. He hoped it was not too late for Liza McAllister.

Chapter 34

Warrant in the breast pocket of his jacket, Detective Sergeant Hannah rang the bell, with Detective Reyes and Sergeant Seaver standing on either side of him.

Hoping for the best, planning for the worst.

What Hannah hadn't expected, though, was to see Lawson McAllister at the door with his quiet counterpart right behind him.

"Hi, Detective Hannah. Have you found my mom?" Lawson asked, his eyes wide with hope.

"No. I'm afraid we're here to ask your father a few questions. Is he here?"

Lawson frowned. "Uh ... no. I already told you he's out of town on business."

"Do you mind if we come in?"

"Sure, please, come in." He stood aside, and the officers entered. "I'm sorry. We saw you guys pull in and thought maybe you had some news about Mom."

"I actually do have news," Hannah said, "but I need to give you this first." He handed over the warrant.

"What's this?" Lawson started reading as his sister looked over his shoulder.

"It's a search warrant to search the premises. We found your mom's truck at MBS. Please step outside while we proceed with the search. Do you need us to explain the warrant and how it works?"

"No, we understand. Pretty simple. This gives you the right to search the property."

Hannah nodded at Detective Reyes and Sergeant Seaver. They began checking the rooms, first searching for Ms. McAllister, and then for any evidence that might point to her whereabouts.

After Hannah escorted the twins outside, he asked them to join him downtown at the department so he could tell them some additional information about the case. His intention was to get a read on if either of these kids were in cahoots with their father or knew more about their mother's abduction than they'd let on.

"Do we have to go downtown? We can talk right here, if that's okay." Alexis had a scared expression on her face. Hannah wasn't sure if it was because she didn't want to go to the LEC or if it was because she had something to hide.

Hannah rocked on his heels, acting like he was thinking about it. "We can talk outside here. But are you sure you don't want to go down to the police department where it's a bit warmer?" It was close to sixty degrees outside, and the breeze was making it feel even chillier.

"We're both okay, if you are, Detective." Lawson didn't look cold, and neither did Alexis, so Hannah nodded.

He said, "As I mentioned, we found your mom's truck, at the airport."

Alexis immediately responded with questions. "So she did make the flight? But where did she go?"

"Please, allow me to finish." Hannah held up his hand to regain control of the questioning.

"Sorry. We're awfully anxious," Alexis said, quietly abashed.

"They searched the surveillance tapes and didn't see your mom enter the airport. Long story short, your father *was* seen at the airport." Hannah took in a deep breath on purpose, to gauge their reactions to that statement before continuing. "We have reason to believe he drove your mom's truck there. We also believe he knows where she is. That he has her."

Stunned silence surrounded them. The twins kept looking at each other and then back at Hannah. Their mouths were practically hanging down to the cement driveway they were standing on. Tears formed in the girl's eyes, threatening to spill over.

Lawson finally managed to say, "I don't understand. Why would Dad take Mom? If he wanted to talk to her, he would go to her office and talk to her."

"We don't know. We are here to investigate the case as it's presented to us." Hannah was getting the impression by their reactions that they were not involved. He softened a bit and said, "Would you like me to call someone for you, to pick you up? This could take a while."

"No, but do you mind if I call our Aunt Trinity?"

"Yes, you can give her a call."

"Thanks. She took the rest of the week off, so she'll probably be able to get us."

"That would be fine. Actually, why don't I drive you over there while we wait for them to finish?" Detective Hannah wanted to speak with Trinity again, in light of the new information pointing to Mr. McAllister as the prime suspect. Where had he taken her, if not back to this house? Did they have other properties, places they used to go, stuff like that? And who better to know that kind of information than a close family friend?

***

Lexi elbowed her brother with a questionable look on her face. Lawson picked up on her gesture but quickly shook his head just once. To tell her *not now* in twin speak. He wrapped his fingers tighter around the piece of paper in his pocket. He needed a little more time to process what he had found. It might mean nothing.

He would keep this close to the vest for now.

***

Trinity Gold sat on the couch in her home, staring at Detective Hannah, when he received a call from Detective Reyes. They had not found Ms. McAllister at the home of her ex-husband, and there was nothing pointing them in any fresh direction. Hannah asked them to wrap up the process, hung up the call, and now politely smiled at Mrs. Gold, waiting for her response to his question.

"I honestly don't know where he could have taken her. To my knowledge, they've never owned a vacation home. They would take family trips up north to the Upper Peninsula, stay in hotels or rental cabins. I can't think of anything else."

"Do you know the names of the places they stayed?"

"No. I don't recall any specifics. If I think of any, I will let you know."

"Did they have family they visited?" He turned to Lawson. "Where are your grandparents located?"

"Dad's parents died before we were born. And we barely knew Mom's parents when they passed away. We were maybe four? I do remember Dad talking about his Gram, and I've seen pictures, but she died before we were born, too."

"Do you know where any of them used to live? Or maybe a family friend of your dad's?"

"Dad mentioned he used to play in the woods at Great Gram's when he was younger. I think that was up north somewhere."

"But you don't remember where that was?"

"No. I don't. I …" Lawson was struggling. Alexis scooted closer to him, wrapped an arm around his shoulder, and then whispered something in his ear. He nodded.

Hannah waited. He looked at Alexis. "And you?"

She shook her head. "I don't remember anything more than Lawson and Aunt Trinity have already said." Then she lowered her eyes to the ground.

Hannah waited a beat more, then slapped his thighs and stood. "Please, try not to worry. We will find her. Thank you for your time."

"Thank you, Detective." Trinity stood to shake his hand.

"I'll see myself out."

As Hannah was closing the door, he heard the emotional release from the trio in the living room. He sighed and hurried down the steps. The clock was ticking to find Ms. McAllister alive. He needed to get back to LEC, see if Mr. McAllister had called. Hopefully, they could trace his location. He'd also have to get a warrant on the phone records for the suspect. The possibility of Liza being alive was growing smaller. He had alerted the ex-husband by calling him. The guy probably thought he had the week to do whatever it was he was doing with her. Now that Hannah had called and left a message ...

Hannah just hoped it hadn't created more problems for Liza McAllister.

When his partner picked up, Hannah said, "Let's head back to LEC and see what we can dig up on another location. And get that warrant for Ledge McAllister's cell phone. Time is of the essence."

Before Hannah could pull out of the driveway, the front door burst open.

"Stop!" Lawson yelled, running across the law with his hands up.

Hannah spiked the brakes and put the car in park. Lawson was pulling a piece of paper out of his front pocket when Hannah exited the car.

"What's this?" Hannah asked as he took the piece of paper from Lawson. Realization dawned on him as he read the barely legible words. He looked up at Lawson.

"I'm sorry, sir. I ... we weren't trying to hide anything. Honest." He pointed at the paper in the detective's hand. "We found it right before you arrived with the warrant. We didn't have time to think about it, what it means or whatever. We weren't trying to defend Dad or hide evidence. It fell out of his jacket in the garage. Honest!" The kid looked terrified, as if he were being hauled off to jail.

Hannah patted Lawson's shoulder and took a minute to digest what had just transpired. He nodded his head toward the house and said, "Let's go back inside." Hannah wanted to find out who else knew about this note. And what they thought about it.

He told Lawson to have a seat in the kitchen, so he couldn't influence Lexi and his "aunt" in any way.

"Lexi, Mrs. Gold, were either of you aware of this?" Hannah handed the note to Mrs. Gold and watched as Lexi sunk a little lower into the couch. Shock registered on Mrs. Gold's face.

"Oh my ..." She didn't finish her sentence. Her hand went to her cheek as she looked over at Lexi. She handed her the note, but Lexi held up her hands and shook her head, as if warding off the plague.

Trinity was visibly perplexed by these actions, as much as by the note. "What ... where ..." She looked at the detective then back again at Lexi. "Did you find this?"

Lexi barely squeaked out, "No. Lawson found it. He said it fell out of Dad's jacket." She threw her hands up over her face and started sobbing.

Lawson appeared from the kitchen, drawn to his anguished twin. Hannah waved his hand to go to her and saw the pain on their aunt's face. Stepping forward and taking the note back from Mrs. Gold, he said, "So, you were unaware they'd found this?"

"I didn't know." Mrs. Gold quieted, and the dark circles under her eyes were on full display as her facial color drained. Tears pooled in her eyes as understanding came to her. "Oh my God. Detective, you have to find her. Now!"

"Couldn't agree more. And that's what we're trying to do. Anything, any little thing, such as this note here … well, it could be important. You see?" He eyeballed the twins for a moment, then back to Trinity. "Now is the time to bring up anything else that comes to mind."

"I have honestly given you all I have. I'll try harder to think of more. But obviously he has her! He has her and …" She stopped herself just as her worried look landed on the twins, who were hanging onto each other for dear life. She took in a deep breath and regained her composure. "Thank you for everything you've done so far, Detective Hannah. We will do more digging and see what we else we can come up with, if anything."

"Good to hear," Hannah said, then headed out the door with renewed determination.

Chapter 35

Liza woke to a blood-curdling scream emanating from somewhere within the house. Blinking her eyes in the dark, her mind registered where she was. She sensed no immediate threats and eased out of the covers. She had a feeling she would find Ledge in the throes of a nightmare.

Ledge was thrashing in the bed, and Liza didn't dare get near him. He was crying and screaming. She couldn't make out the words. She crept into the room and waited to see if he came out of it on his own. Two minutes later, and it continued. Her inner caregiver couldn't take it any longer. She reached the edge of the bed, turned on the lamp at the bed, and tried soothing words to calm him. He slowed as if he'd heard her. She continued with the calming method she had used when his night terrors had been bad early on in their marriage.

He seemed to be relaxing. The screaming had stopped, but his face was still fraught with worry. When she thought he would go back to a restful sleep, Ledge reached out and grabbed her arm. She screamed, and Ledge's eyes flew open, pulling her into the bed with him. He rolled her under him. Liza screamed his name over and over, "Ledge! Ledge! It's me, Lizabeth. Wake up, Ledge!"

Ledge stared at her, unseeing, and wrapped his hands around her throat. She couldn't breathe. His weight was now shifted to her midsection as his viselike grip threatened to end her life. Somewhere within her dimming sight, she remembered a technique from her self-defense class. She threw her arms into action and was able to break his hold on her neck before she lost consciousness. That left Ledge off balance, and she used that to her benefit.

Ledge flopped over onto the mattress, and Liza moved quickly to get as far away from him as she could. Grasping her bruised neck, she looked back at the bed to make sure he stayed there and wasn't on his way back for another attack. Breathing in much-needed air, she saw he wasn't moving, but his chest was rising and falling in a rapid manner. She watched as she regained control of her own breathing. Seeing that he was not going to continue his onslaught of rage against her, she backed out of the room.

*****

Ledge raked his hands through his wet hair as he stumbled to the bathroom. He hadn't remembered leaving his nightstand light on. What had happened during his nightmare?

As he stared at himself in the mirror over the sink, it all came back to him suddenly. Vivid waves of images rushed at him like a tidal wave. Were they real? He was trying to choke Lizabeth! The light in her eyes was fading! The harder he tried to remove his hands, the tighter the grip got on her neck.

What the hell had he done?

No, no, it wasn't real. Couldn't be real. Though he had heard her soothing words, like she used to do whenever he had nightmares about his brother's accident. Was that a distant memory, or had it actually happened?

Tears sprung to his eyes. Damn, he needed help. He knew that. He needed to get home and get back to his real life, with his wife by his side to guide his recovery.

The Ledge staring him back in the mirror was exhausted. All these memories in this house were consuming him. He realized too late that he should have chosen a better location to reunite with his wife. He turned on the faucet and splashed cold water on his face a few times to clear the remnants of the terror. After drying himself off and taking a few calming breaths, he felt a little better.

He turned the light off and tiptoed down the hall to check on Lizabeth. He needed to make sure she was okay. He prayed his nightmare hadn't woken her. From the looks of the bed, he'd thrashed around quite a bit and was surprised he hadn't landed on the floor. Some nights his abrupt falls on the hardwood floors had woken him in the past. Peeking into Lizabeth's room, he saw she was covered and quiet. He silently entered the room and let the hall light fall on her face. She was sleeping. Suddenly feeling lost, he settled in the chair next to her bed. Leaning forward, he said a silent prayer that she stayed safe. She was his world, and he would be utterly lost without her.

The tears streamed down his face. He wiped them away and kept his eyes on his wife. Watching her sleep gave him the peace he needed. Finally, he pulled himself out of the chair and left his angel. He knew he needed more sleep. He prayed it would be peaceful this time around. It had been a long quiet day, and they had gone to bed early. Both of them were exhausted. He needed to seal the deal with her tomorrow. No matter what. Time was up.

Chapter 36

Detective Hannah was impatiently waiting for the cell-phone company to release the suspect's phone data and ping locations. They had also issued an APB on the suspect's car. Hannah was sitting at his desk when Detective Reyes walked in with two cups of coffee and sandwiches from the deli down the street. Hannah grunted his appreciation, opened his sandwich, and scarfed it down. He'd skipped breakfast to get going on the investigation early. Time was ticking, and the process was moving slower than he liked.

His email chimed, and he set his coffee down to click on the message. "Hot damn! It's the phone records." He hit "print" and then went over to the printer to retrieve them. Walking back, he was already looking at the first page. He saw a number that stood out to him. Pulling out his notepad, he compared the numbers that he had listed there and saw that it was Lawson's phone number. Then there was another that showed up frequently earlier in the month. He reached for his highlighter and highlighted that number. There was not much activity for the summer. The records were only five pages, and most every call was either to work or to one of his kids.

Except for that one number.

"Well, I'll check this phone number," he said to Reyes, pointing at the highlighted number. "It's not from this area. There are six calls received and dialed to this number earlier this month, over a period of a few days."

Reyes gave him a thumbs-up. "Sounds promising."

Hannah changed his phone settings so that his own number would show up as a private one, and then the mystery number. After five rings, the call was forwarded to voicemail.

"Hi, you've reached Bill, owner of Bill's Handyman & Repair. Please leave a message with your phone number, and I'll get back to ya."

Hannah left a message, asking Bill to call back. Looking at Reyes, he said, "Can you research Bill's Handyman & Repair and see where's he's located?"

Reyes nodded. "Can do."

Hannah tossed his sandwich wrapper and now-empty coffee cup in the trash. He came around to Reye's desk and looked over his shoulder as he clicked on the Facebook page that had led to Bill's Handyman & Repair page. Reyes clicked on the "About" information. The guy was listed in West Branch.

They looked at each other for a long few seconds. Reyes spoke first. "Why would he need a handyman from West Branch? The house was in good repair when we went through it this morning."

"Why, indeed? Unless he has another house in that area. The kids didn't recall anything about another house." Before Hannah could even ask, Reyes looked up the phone number for the police in that area.

Hannah walked back to his desk and saw another email from the phone company. This time with a list of the pings from that phone. He printed the list—it was surprisingly long.

"Well, well, well. Mr. McAllister has been very busy over the past few months. He's been traveling back and forth to West Branch regularly," he said to Reyes. "We have a location ping last night at 10:38 p.m. off a tower near West Branch. So he's there, or at least *was* there last night."

Hannah then grabbed the phone records; he hadn't focused on the times the suspect had called and texted the kids, only the phone numbers. Looking at the last page, he glanced at the last call made. It was at 10:40 p.m. to his son. The call had lasted only three and a half minutes.

"Okay, Reyes, we definitely need to be talking to the cops up there. And the handyman, Bill."

"Call's in to the handyman already. Just have to wait for him to call back. And here's the main number to the police in that area."

Hannah held up a hand. "You call them. I'm going to call the son. Let's go see him again, in fact. He didn't tell us his father had called him last night, or earlier, from the looks of this record. He didn't even mention that he'd been in touch with him at all."

Reyes rubbed his chin. "Odd. Let's do it."

Hannah picked up his cell phone and dialed Lawson's cell number. Lawson picked up on the second ring.

"Detective, have you heard anything?"

"Actually, we have some new information. Are you still at the house?"

"Yes, I was getting ready for class."

"Hold off on that. I'll be right over."

"Uh, okay. See you soon."

Hannah hung up, looked at Reyes, who was on the phone with a department in West Branch. While he waited for the call to finish, he reviewed Saturday's ping records. They were near the airport and a tower near Ms. McAllister's residence.

Reyes said, "I'm going to email them the business website page that has McAllister's picture on it. It's the Ogemaw sheriff's office that serves that area, by the way."

"I'll wait while you do that. The son is still at the house. I told him we'd be right over."

Reyes tapped a few keys. "Done. Let's go see what he has to say."

Grabbing the phone records from his desk, Hannah folded them and placed them in his shirt pocket.

***

Lawson was feeling so many emotions when he answered the door to Hannah and Reyes. The detectives didn't look happy, and that worried him even more.

"So, what is the new information? Does it lead to my mom?"

Lexi entered the room, silently as usual, and sat next to her brother.

"Yes, but you failed to tell us you'd been in touch with your father. More than once."

"Oh, I'm sorry. I totally forgot." Lawson looked like he'd been called into the principal's office.

Lexi looked at her brother with wide eyes but then jumped in to protect him. "It was before you told us that Dad might have taken Mom. We were upset, and Lawson wanted to talk to him."

Hannah gave her a dismissive look and turned back to Lawson. "What did you and your father discuss?" Glaring at Lexi, he added, "Especially during the second call, which was *after* you knew we were looking at him for taking your mom." Hannah pulled himself up to his full height to exaggerate his position of control in the room. Lawson's mouth opened and closed in the nervous fervor of a bass out of water. When he could form words, they flowed like a rushing river.

"I called him because we were both panicked. We didn't know what to do, and he didn't answer his phone, so I told him to call me. When I *did* hear from him, it was late Tuesday, but it was a text that said he'd call the next morning. Wednesday. Uh, yesterday."

Lawson took a breath before continuing. "So, he called me yesterday morning, but he said he had a meeting, was checking in on us, and then asked about Mom and what you had asked me about. I told him that you had said I was the last one she'd talked to before she went missing." His voice cracked on the last part of that sentence, and Alexis rubbed his back. He said in a quiet voice, "I'm sorry. I'm having a hard time believing Dad took her ... even after finding that note. Anyway, he told me not to worry, and then he was called into a meeting. He said he'd check back in last night."

"When did he call you last night? And what did he say?"

"It was after 10:30. He asked how we were doing and if we'd heard anything about Mom. I said we were okay but had heard nothing about Mom. And I asked him how things were going and when he'd be back." Lawson broke down, and Lexi grabbed the tissues from the coffee table.

Lawson wiped his eyes. "Sorry."

"Take your time. Anything you can remember might help us find her."

"I remember he said he was going to try to come home Friday, that the meetings had gone well. I think he also said something about it depended upon flights, too."

Reyes and Hannah exchanged glances. Hannah took another tack. "So, how do you think your dad knew your mom was going on a cruise?"

Lawson looked at Lexi. They were both shaking their heads. He said, "We never told him she was going on a cruise. No need for him to know what she was doing; I mean, they're divorced. We were at school, doing our thing mostly. I did tell him she was missing, you know, on the phone. Like I said. But he never mentioned anything about her being on a cruise. And until we found that note yesterday, we had no idea he'd even known." Lawson paused and looked at Lexi with an exasperated expression. "This makes so much more sense when you think about the note and Dad's lack of interest in Mom being missing."

"Have you mentioned anything about it since then? The cruise?"

Both Lawson and Lexi shook their heads again. "Never. Plus, Mom asked us not to say anything about it to Dad. She was adamant we not give him any information about her personal life. Or anything about her, really." He shrugged and wiped his nose. After a few minutes, his eyes brightened, as if he'd just had a moment of clarity. "You know, I thought this was odd." He scrolled through his phone. "Here. This is what Dad texted me after I left him a voicemail, on Tuesday."

Hannah took the phone and read the text, and then pulled his own cell phone out to snap a picture of the text:

Sorry I missed you, son. I will call you at home tomorrow morning. You both get some sleep. I can't get away right now. Things are going better than I'd hope for, and this meeting is headed into a late evening. I'm sure your mom is fine. You know how she likes to take time for herself and doesn't always check in. I'm getting called back into the meeting. Talk in the morning. Love, Dad

Hannah looked up at Lawson and handed back his cell phone. "Thank you, I appreciate your honesty. Next time he calls, please let me know."

"Will do, sir."

"One more question. Has your dad had any repair work done recently to the home?"

"No. Why do you ask?"

"Wanted to make sure we weren't missing anything. How did your dad sound last night?"

"Tired ... but he seemed okay," Lawson said after some thought.

"We'll be on our way. Thank you for your time." He and Reyes stood.

"Thank you, Detective. We'll let you know if we hear from Dad tonight. I'm not sure if he will call, actually. He didn't really say. Only that he was going to try to be home tomorrow." Then something else seemed to strike Lawson. "I …we never knew he had an out-of-town meeting. And that seemed strange to me, but Lexi reminded me he hasn't been himself since the divorce. And, of course, we were always studying. Still, Dad always tells us when he has a business trip. Always. I thought it was strange. And last night, Dad still thought she was taking time to herself and that she would show up eventually. If he took her, then maybe that's why he's downplaying her disappearance." His face washed with guilt the moment he said the words, and Hannah felt for the kid. Especially when the sister gave him a sour look.

Hannah decided to cut to the chase. "I'm afraid the evidence *is* leading to him. Listen, you've both been very helpful. If your dad calls again, call me. We need to get to your mom before … anything happens."

That statement sobered Lawson. Lexi put a hand to her mouth to suppress a gasp.

This was serious business. Dangerous business.

***

Hannah asked Reyes to call the sheriff in Ogemaw County while they drove back to the department. He wanted to see if they'd received Reyes's email and if they recognized McAllister. It was going on four in the afternoon, and they were running out of daylight. He didn't want to be traipsing around in the dark, but they would if they had to. Time was running out; he could feel it. Day Six in a case like this would not have a good outcome.

When they got back to HQ, Hannah checked his messages and then called the clerk to ask if Mr. McAllister had returned his call. He had not. "Not making yourself any less of a suspect here, Mr. McAllister."

Reyes nodded his head in agreement and said, "I spoke with Deputy Bryant in Crawford County. He mentioned the sergeant on duty was out assisting on a call that had come in. Bryant said he'd have him call back as soon as he returned. I gave him my cell phone again. He also said they viewed McAllister's picture, and it was not someone he recognized himself nor had anyone there in the department. I'll try calling the handyman again and see if I get through this time."

Hannah nodded and headed to grab some coffee for both of them. He could hear Reyes leave another message for the handyman. After so many hits, they were striking out at the moment. Not an option.

He handed Reyes his coffee. "Until either of them calls us back, we're stuck. Let's run through the property records online and see if we can find any other property in Mr. McAllister's name. Maybe that will help us even before anyone calls us back."

Reyes gave a thumbs-up. "On it." Right then, his cell phone rang. "Detective Reyes."

"This is Sheriff Ross from the Crawford County Sheriff's Department. As you heard from Deputy Bryant, no one here recognizes the guy. I have the BOLO on the suspect's car, and one of the deputies is searching the area to see if it's parked anywhere up here."

"Thank you, Sheriff. By chance, do you know a Bill from Bill's Handyman & Repair? We've left him two messages and haven't heard back from him."

"Oh, yeah. We all know Bill. The man does fine work. What do you want with him?"

"Our suspect has been in contact with him a few times over the past two months. We have reason to believe that maybe he's hired him to do some work."

"I'll drive out to Bill's. I'll take the picture with me and see if he recognizes him. If he does, I'll call you back."

"Much obliged. Thank you, Sheriff Ross."

"You betcha." Ross hung up.

Reyes said, "Well, maybe there's the break we need."

Chapter 37

Lawson and Lexi watched their aunt and uncle making calls as they sat there in silence. Time was slipping away, and they had exhausted their abilities to assist. If the police had found anything during their warrant search, they weren't saying. No news was not always good news. And Lawson didn't dare to call his Dad again.

Lexi got up from her perch next to him and headed toward the bathroom. Aunt Trinity hung up her phone and walked back into the kitchen where Uncle Ollie was still talking to someone on the other end. No one they had contacted today had garnered any more information to point the detectives in the right direction. Here it was evening, and the moon was starting to poke out for the long journey to daybreak. Lawson's skin was crawling from sitting still. He stood up and started pacing around the living room. Then he heard Uncle Ollie say, "Yes, we'll stay in touch." Lawson marched to the kitchen to find out if any "new" news had been discovered.

Ollie was holding Trinity in a hug when he saw Lawson approach. Ollie shook his head no, his expression grim.

Deflated, Lawson plopped into a chair at the kitchen table. That had been their last call—another road to nowhere. He dropped his head to the table and sent up a silent prayer that his Mom was safe and that they'd find her unharmed. Lexi found her way to the room and came up behind her twin, wrapping her arms around him.

Trinity separated from her husband and wiped the wetness from her eyes. Ollie straightened and looked around the room, fists clenched as if his frustration had turned a corner into rage at feeling so helpless. Lawson understood. It was exactly how he was feeling.

***

Ollie was at a loss as to what to do to console everyone and provide the answers they all needed, but most of all, he felt completely responsible for Liza's disappearance. He should have seen it coming. He should have been able to see Ledge was up to something and put a stop to it before this. He snatched his phone off the counter and stalked to the garage. He needed to breathe, to regroup. To not lose hope.

He picked up the whiskey bottle to pour himself a quick shot and stopped halfway to the small glass on the bar top. A memory flickered into his vision. He stared at the glass of liquid in his hand for a few seconds and then twisted the top back on the bottle and slammed it down. He wanted to throw the bottle across the room to hear it smash against the wall, but that was not going to solve anything. He was almost one-hundred-percent sure it was his fault that Ledge had found Liza. Glancing back at the bottle on the bench, he remembered the last time he had been out here—with Ledge, the day the girls were celebrating the divorce. It was his fault. Ledge had left right after Ollie had almost spilled the beans. In fact, he was sure the beans had been spilled. Ledge had caught on and tracked Liza.

As he thought through that evening from that summer night, he remembered Ledge saying he needed to leave, but his phone had never made a sound. He had faked the call; Ollie was sure of it.

Ollie took out his phone, intending to call Ledge and call him out. But he hesitated, ultimately returning the cell to his pocket as a chill ran through him. If he called Ledge and somehow pushed him further … no, he didn't want to push that button.

Damn it, Ledge!

He pulled back his fist, ready to punch the wall, when Trinity popped into the garage.

"Ollie!" she shouted.

He stopped his fist in midair, turned his head, and lowered his arm. Shock was plastered all over her face. She approached him slowly and held her hands out for him to come to her. She was never one to scare easy. *My Rock.* He held his hand out to her and eased into her arms. So soothing, her embrace. *Funny how you think you're the strong one and then, you find that right woman and realize you were never that strong without her.* Relief washed over him. He'd be lost without her.

He was struck by that thought, realizing that was probably the same feeling Ledge had been experiencing without Liza. But Ledge going to this extreme—and all avenues were pointing in that direction … well, Ollie was not sure he could forgive him for that.

Trinity pulled back from him and looked him over with gentle eyes. With a faint smile on her face, she gave him a quick kiss on his cheek. "I don't think the kids should go back to that empty house tonight."

"Agreed." Ollie released his wife and turned her toward the door to head back into the house. He felt a little better. Shaking his head, he tried to remove the guilt he felt. He needed to stay focused, for his family's sake. Being angry with himself was not going to solve anything.

Chapter 38

Detective Hannah walked into his dark home after punching in the security code. His life as a detective was a lonely one. His wife had left him after nine years of marriage and had taken their ten-year-old daughter. It had been almost two years now since they left, and a year since the divorce had been settled. Even still, his ex-wife was eternally angry with him. He saw their daughter every other weekend when he wasn't called in on a case. Every time he had to tell her he couldn't pick up Madison, Crystal would throw it in his face—that she *still* had to deal with his job, even though they weren't married. But he wouldn't apologize for working his dream job, his calling. The puzzles, clues, and finding the answers were what had drawn him into the world of police work.

Still, he knew all too well that his adorable little clone of her mother would soon become a teenager who didn't want anything to do with either of her parents. He savored the remaining pre-teen moments they had left, and this weekend was one of them.

Hannah removed his blue blazer and hung it on the back of the kitchen chair. Glancing at the microwave, he saw it was after 8:30 p.m. He pulled a Michelob Light from the fridge, wandered into the living room, and turned the TV on for some background noise. He hadn't tried to have more than a few dates with anyone else. The job pulled you in and swallowed you whole. There was no room for error. You also had to have a partner that you could trust and rely on to have your back. Crystal had not been that partner. In reality, after the love-lust cleared from his eyes, he knew she was nothing more than a selfish, cold woman. He thanked God she was a decent mother.

He slumped down on the couch and absently flipped through the channels, not paying any attention to the shows that flashed across the screen. He had yet to pop the top on the cold beer in his hand, when his phone rang.

"Hannah."

"Detective, this is Sheriff Ross up here in Ogemaw County. Bill finally made it home, and he's headed over here to look at your suspect's picture and give us any information he can. In fact, he's already told us that he remembers working with a Mr. McAllister recently on a kitchen remodel. He can tell us how to get to him. How fast can you get a warrant and get up here?"

Hannah sat upright like a bolt of lightning had hit him in the ass. "En route now to get the warrant. Send me the location as soon as the handyman gets it for you. I looked up the drive to your department earlier, and it's close to an hour away. I think I can make it in forty after we get the warrant signed."

"I've called the local MSP. They're getting SWAT together, so they'll be ready when you get here."

"See you then."

Hannah hung up before Ross could reply and was dialing Reyes to see if he was able to go. He had flipped the TV off with the phone to his ear, grabbing his jacket and sprinting to the garage.

"Reyes."

"You able to go north? They know where the suspect is, or at least the location of the remodeling."

"Ready now. You want to pick me up here or meet at the LEC?"

"Your house is on the way, so I'll be at your place in three."

"I'll be at the end of the driveway."

Hannah hung up as he threw the switch for his red flashing light on his car and raced to Reyes's house. As promised, his partner was standing at the end of the driveway, Go Bag in hand. He hopped in, and Hannah was pulling away before the door was shut. "Bill, the handyman, called Ross back." He gave Reyes the details of his phone call with Sheriff Ross, finishing with, "Ross called their Michigan State Police Department up there, and they're assembling SWAT. It should go quickly after we get there with the papers."

"Let's hope the vic is there, and we made it in time."

"Call it in. Get the warrant."

"On it."

Reyes placed the call into LEC to let them know where they were headed and that they needed the papers ASAP. Hannah pushed the pedal harder, traveling the fastest route to the department. He threw another prayer up to heaven, asking that this case ended well.

Luck was on their side that night. The papers had been signed by the time they arrived at the department. That rarely happened. Hannah hoped that was a good sign. The two detectives raced back to the car and headed toward West Branch like bats out of hell. Hannah silently prayed that they'd not hit any critters along the way. A deer accident would greatly hinder their precious time.

He said, "You know, Reyes ... I don't know if the target's location is within the city limits or out of town. But we want everyone alive, so we'll follow SWAT's lead."

"Agreed. Wife won't want any other results."

"Right."

Hannah pulled into the Ogemaw County Sheriff's Department near the edge of West Branch. Reyes grabbed his bag from the back seat while Hannah popped the trunk to get his own. They walked in and were buzzed back into the offices. The deputy escorted them back and announced their arrival to Sheriff Ross, who was standing at the front of the desk, waiting for them to arrive. Randy Ross was a tall wall of a man. Built to handle anything a criminal threw at him. He stood over six feet tall. His graying brown hair, nearly a buzz cut, gave him the look of a distinguished and knowledgeable sheriff.

"Sheriff Ross, I'm Detective Hannah." He threw his hand forward to begin the niceties and get them out of the way. Everyone followed suit. Handyman Bill was the last to be introduced. Hannah zeroed in on him. He was an older man with gray-white hair. He stood tall next to the Sheriff, not quite meeting Ross's full height. He must have been working late, as he still had sawdust on his clothes.

Hannah said, "Can you men bring us up to speed?

Ross rubbed his hands together and said, "Right. SWAT was here to meet with Bill, and we have about five minutes before we leave to meet

SWAT. Bill, please tell him what you know." Ross stepped back and leaned against the wall.

"The man in the picture there is Mr. McAllister. He hired me to help him renovate a kitchen about fifteen minutes northeast from here. He said it had been his grandparents' house, and he wanted to bring it back to life. He showed me the plans, and he already had most of it done, actually. He needed help lifting the cabinets and setting them into place. He also needed help bringing in the appliances. The place didn't look like it'd seen anyone for a few decades. It's set back in the woods about two hundred feet or so from the road. The driveway isn't a straight shot. It winds a bit to the right." Bill pointed at a yellow tablet of paper; a rough draft of the location had been drawn on it. The drive came in from the south, and an outbuilding was on the right as you pulled in, house on the left.

Bill ran his finger along the drawing and stopped at the main house. "There's the front door that takes you through the living room, and to the right is the kitchen. There's a wraparound porch that leads around the kitchen to the back door, which is the entrance to a small mudroom. Those were the only two external doors I'm aware of. I had to use the restroom there, and there are three bedrooms at the south end of the house. At least, I counted three doors, and I'm guessing they're bedrooms." Pointing at another room, he said, "I think that's the dining room. It has double doors to it, sliding into the wall, and I never saw the inside of that room."

"How was the suspect when you dealt with him?"

The handyman chewed his lip for a moment, then said, "Well, he was quick to anger when something didn't go right. A perfectionist. Wanted everything precise and level. He seemed to be holding back, almost like he bit his tongue a lot while I was there. I almost told him I was done, that he could find someone else, but he seemed to calm down the closer we got to finishing the project." He paused and shook his head. "You know, I've worked with hotheads before, but this guy had a meanness about him. I don't know how to describe it, other than he was dark. Almost demonic-looking when the vein in his neck bulged and his eyes clouded over. Then he'd shake it off and would be fine again. I've never seen anything like it. I was glad to be done with him."

Hannah nodded. "Thank you, Bill. You've been very helpful."

"Happy to help." He nodded and left the room with one of the deputies.

The sheriff nodded at the remaining deputy in the room. "Lewis, tell Detective Hannah what you discovered today."

"I was the one who took the picture around to local businesses and all the hangouts here. I wasn't having much luck until I spoke with the clerk at the Handy Mart. Small grocery store around here. She recognized him. He was there on Monday. I asked her if he'd purchased anything. She said he'd purchased a few double-sided dead bolts, some food items, and cleaning supplies. Said he wore a ball cap, too, one that kind of covered his eyes, but she knew it was him because she thinks he's hot and was trying to make a move on him ... until she saw his wedding ring."

"Did she mention anything else? Did she see him drive away?" Hannah asked.

"No, she didn't see his car, and I checked the surveillance tapes. They do go back to Monday, but he must have known where they were located because he hid his face from the view of the cameras."

"Thank you, Deputy Lewis. Guys, we need to change, and then we'll be ready to go." Hannah picked up his Go Bag and nodded at Reyes.

Ross said, "Lewis will show you where you can change. SWAT is waiting for us."

"We won't take long." Hannah and Reyes followed Lewis to another room in the department to get changed into their tactical gear. Suits were not needed where they were headed.

Chapter 39

Liza held her breath and made her way down the hall, purposely avoiding the squeaky floorboard she'd found the day before. The earlier altercation had left her reeling. Her throat hurt, and she was sure she had bruises from his hands, but she wasn't going to take the time to check. She prayed that he was finally sound asleep. As she approached his room, she heard snoring. She listened for movement but heard none. Liza took a step directly into the doorway and, thanks to the moonlight coming through the open curtains, confirmed that he was deep into the throes of sleep. No thrashing or screaming. Liza touched her sore neck and exited the bedroom, to go change her clothes.

She hustled to the kitchen, grabbed a chair, and made her way to the mudroom door. She stood still for a moment and listened again. It was dissonantly quiet. She entered the mudroom with the chair and set it in front of the exit door. She climbed up on the chair, found the key, and gently stepped to the ground, thankful she hadn't tripped or fallen so far.

Her heart was hammering hard in her chest as she waited for Ledge to appear in all his anger. But he never came. She turned the lock on the doorknob and placed the key in the dead bolt. She opened the door. This time, she would make good on her escape plan. Failure was not an option. She touched her throat again. The images from earlier fueling her to flee.

She headed straight for the barn, where she was certain Ledge's car was. It was a bitter night, and her lungs burned from the short distance she'd run. She turned the cold knob of the side door to the barn, and it opened. *Thank you, God!*

She searched around on the wall and found the light switch. She flipped the switch on and made the mistake of looking up as the lights buzzed to life. She was momentarily blinded. After she blinked away the light strobes in her vision, she gasped in relief with a small victory happy dance. There it was. Ledge's car.

She slid into the driver's seat and searched for the key in the ignition. Nothing. She searched the cup holders, the center console, under the mats. Still. No. Keys.

She pulled down the visor, but the only thing there was a sealed envelope addressed to no one. She put that back and got out of the car to check around the seats. Nothing. She got back in on the passenger's side and opened the glove box, only to find a few napkins, insurance card, and registration.

"Damn it! Why did you pick now to listen to me about not leaving your keys in the car?"

She got back out of the car and looked around at the walls. The workbench. Keys. Where would he put his keys? Maybe he really had taken them inside.

She wanted to punch something. She'd made it out, but now she was stuck walking in the frigid air or …

She stopped. Maybe there was another vehicle. She saw the side door that led to the north side of the barn. She half jogged to it, turned the handle … and it opened. She thanked God yet again. Walking inside, she saw moonlight streaming in from the old barn walls. But that wasn't enough to illuminate the large object she could see shadowed twenty feet away from her. She felt to her right along the old wooden walls for a light switch. Finding it, she flipped it on and saw the large item—an old red tractor. But it had a front blade on it. *That's not going to help me.*

She pulled open drawers and cabinets along the wall separating the two parts of the barn. Moved stuff around. No keys. No more time. She had to hoof it to the road. It was her only option now.

***

Ledge woke up from another nightmare. He was covered in sweat, and he clung to the sheets and his night clothes. He hoped he hadn't woken Lizabeth. He yanked his feet out of the tangled mess of sheets and sat on the edge of the bed. Raking his hands through his damp hair, he pulled himself together and got up to get a drink from the kitchen. The moonlight shone in from the living room windows, and he was glad he had left the curtains pulled back. The curtains had shrunk after washing them earlier that day, but they had held together, and he was still able to pull them shut if he needed to. The fact that the curtains were messed up had bothered him, but he had held it together—for Lizabeth's sake, of course.

He reached the fridge and took out a bottle of water, drank half of it, then walked over to the kitchen window. All was calm outside. He finished his water and was about to turn around and throw the bottle away when a light came on in the barn. He saw it shining through the wood slats.

What the hell …?

It took him only a second to figure out what was going on. He tossed the bottle toward the trash bin, missed it, and ignored the urge to pick it up. He ran down the hall to Gram's room. She was gone. Again.

He ran to his room, ripped off his drenched sleepwear, and yanked on a pair of jeans, grabbed a sweatshirt, and slammed his feet into his shoes—without socks.

He was already hot from the nightmare and didn't take the time to try to find a coat. He ran to the back door and felt for the key. Just as he had thought. It was gone. And the door was locked.

He rushed to the craft room, where he kept his keys, and then to the front door. Jamming the key in the dead bolt, he flipped it around, nearly breaking the key off in the lock, and jerked the door open.

He rushed outside, not bothering to close the door. His mind and heartbeat raced. He had the car keys, so she wasn't leaving in that. But who knew where she'd end up if he didn't get to her before she got out of the barn. He zoned out with tunnel vision, focused only on the door of the shop.

"Lizabeth! Are you going somewhere?" The Demon loudly goaded her while making his way to the barn in record time.

The light had been turned out in the barn just before he called out. He reached the shop and found the door locked. He banged on it, screaming, "Lizabeth, a lock won't stop me!" He pulled his keys out of his pocket, thankful he hadn't left them in the dead bolt of the front door in his hurry. He fumbled for the right key and finally was able to turn the knob.

He entered the dark shop and shut the door, locking it behind him. There was only one way in and one way out, and that would slow her down if she got past him. He flipped on the lights and searched the shop, even looking under the bench for her small frame. Then he opened the door and looked inside the car. She wasn't there. "Come out, come out, wherever you are, *Sugar Bear*. You can't hide from me. I know your scent. I know the way you think. I will find you," he hissed.

Chapter 40

Liza's breathing was ragged, and she tried to slow her heart rate so she could listen, but the blood was rushing through her ears like a freight train. She'd never felt so frightened in all her life. She had almost made it to the shop door when she heard him holler across the driveway. She hurriedly locked the door, flipped off the light, and retraced her steps as fast as she could to get back to the walkway door that separated the barn from the shop.

She hoped she could remember the layout well enough to hide in the dark. She had not seen another walkway door into the old barn, and the tall sliding barn doors on the front of the barn were locked from the inside with a chain and a padlock that she obviously didn't have a key to. *I knew I should have run down the driveway. I could have hidden in the brush. Should have, could have ...* Liza chastised herself as she made it up the stairs to the loft. She heard Ledge tearing things apart in his grandpa's old shop. Then she heard him call out to her, mocking her in that evil voice the Demon used.

Ledge was gone. The Demon had arrived.

"Lizabeth, I smell your fear. You can't hide from me."

He taunted her as he closed in. Chills ran through her body, and she almost shook the box next to her. He was now in the barn and had turned on the lights. Having no other options, she hunkered down in the loft. She kept breathing in through her nose and out through her mouth to get herself calmed down. She pulled her defense classes back into the forefront of her mind as she listened to the Demon yank the old cabinets and appliances around the floor of the barn, throwing them out of his way, huffing from his exertion.

She saw her own breath in the air and stuck her mouth inside her sweatshirt to hide it, in case he came up the stairs. *Of course he'll come up the stairs, you idiot!* She felt like she was in a bad horror movie. She wedged herself between a bushy old Christmas tree and a dusty box. The sneeze took her by surprise, but she squelched it and prayed he didn't hear the tiny sound. She listened, feeling like her ears were on fire from the effort, but heard no grunting or footsteps heading her way.

She hoped she was small enough that she wouldn't be seen in her hidey-hole. This location gave her enough room to race back to the stairs if he passed by her.

"Lizabeth, I know you're in here. Make it easy on yourself and come out."

She stayed as still as she could. The mocking voice sent shivers down her spine again. His words insinuated he might let her live if she came out now. She knew better. The Demon was not to be trusted. She held her stance and heard footsteps on the stairs. She slowed her breathing the best she could and froze when she heard him on the landing.

"I know you're up here, Lizabeth. I see your footprints on the stairs."

Shit! Can I have just a little bit of luck, a little bit of a break, please? She hoped her footprints were not visible on the loft floor in this dim light, or he'd follow them around until he found her hiding place. She heard him pulling boxes over and making his point very clear as to what mood he was in. He was on the railing side of the loft, and she was hunkered down directly across from him. She hazarded a glance and saw that he'd stopped moving. He was opening a box.

He's opening a freaking box?

Liza realized the box was large enough for her to hide inside, and he was checking every possible spot.

Go Fish, Demon.

She couldn't see what was in the box, but it had stopped him in his tracks. She thought about running, but he was still too close to her. If he would move farther toward the back of the loft, she could race to the stairs, knocking the big Christmas tree in his way, slide down the rusty metal railing of the stairs, and make it to the door. *IF.*

She watched the Demon pull clothes out of the box. He kneaded his hands in what looked like a child's sweater. She couldn't see his face, but all of a sudden, he wailed out a loud cry and threw the sweater across the loft, narrowly missing her in the process. She wanted to duck her head down, but she'd become riveted by what she was seeing. He'd grabbed more clothing items from the box and vigorously tossed them over the railing. He tossed entire boxes of stuff, too. His wailing was loud and beastly. Like a wounded animal that had been snared in a trap.

Ledge made his way down the railing until all the boxes were gone on that side of the loft. He turned, and the tears on his face were visible as he raged on, grabbing more boxes. She heard him scream John's name as he cried. Realization dawned on her that the boxes of clothes were his brother's.

Feeling just a smidgeon of pain for him, she bit her lip. Then she realized now was the moment. She needed to make her move before he got to her hiding place. He was far enough back at the end of the loft now.

Time to go.

Her exit wasn't graceful, as her legs were numb from the position she'd been holding. She tripped over the Christmas tree branches that had been hiding her and shoved them to the side to make a run for the stairs.

The Demon grunted, and she heard him coming fast across the loft in her direction. Only five steps from the stairs, he caught up to her, picked her up, and spun her around so fast she almost vomited. She had pins and needles in her legs, and she thought her ribs were going to break under the force of his grip. She couldn't breathe. When he slowed, she looked down at his tear-stained face. The veins in his neck were bursting, and his black eyes were unseeing.

She knew she was dead. From somewhere, she heard a scream. Then she realized it was her own voice, throwing out her battle cry. She jammed her thumbs into the Demon's eyes. He cried out and dropped her.

She fell to the floor of the loft like a sack of potatoes, then scrambled to get up and head for the stairs. Ledge stomped down on her foot, still rubbing his right eye. She felt the pain, like fire, run up her left ankle. He bent down to scoop her up again.

Hell no! She threw out her other leg and connected with his bad knee. He howled in agony as he fell backward and clutched his leg.

Who's playing dirty pool now, fucker! She knew he'd injured that knee in high school on the field. She tried to stand back up, but the pain in her foot was so strong she feared he'd broken it.

The Demon reached out and snatched her left ankle out from under her, and she fell hard again, whacking her elbow against the floor. Then it was her cheek, as her teeth rammed together as he let go of her ankle. She was stunned into stillness until the meaty paw of the Demon grabbed her again, even as he lay on the floor, and dragged her back toward the center of the loft, toward him. Her belly burned with fresh splinters. She feared death was near. Grunting heavily, he pulled himself upright, keeping her ankle in his hand. He rolled her over to face him. His eyes were teared up from the damage she'd inflicted … and probably his mental anguish, too. The searing pain in her left ankle kept her from being able to kick his hand away from her other foot.

What could she use to protect herself? She frantically looked around for something to grab and throw at him or stab him with. There was nothing in reach as she struggled against his vise-like grip.

The Demon had regained his composure and was staring directly at her. His nostrils flared, and his breathing was ragged. He was bent over her, sneering. His breath was visible in the chilled air as he screamed at her, "You fucking bitch! You will never leave me. You don't get to leave me. *You are mine forever!*" And with that, he released her ankle and leaned forward to try to grab her by the hair. It was a long enough time for her to pull her good leg back to her chest. Letting out a scream, Liza kicked the Demon square in the chest with everything she had left in her.

Ledge stumbled backward and tried to regain his balance by grabbing the rail of the loft.

She heard the wood snap, and she gasped.

He fell through the rickety old railing, screaming all the way down to the barn floor.

"Holy shit. Holy shit. Oh my God. Oh…" She panted out the words as she crawled to the edge of the loft. Peered over.

He'd landed on the blade of the tractor below, his head and body in positions they shouldn't be. A dark pool was seeping out from beneath him.

Before she could fully grasp the scene below her, a loud crash came from the shop area. She heard someone holler, "Search warrant!" Rushed footsteps scuttled across the cement shop floor, and then bodies clad in dark clothes and guns burst through the walkway door of the barn. Liza stared at them, emotions flooding her body. The tears suddenly rushed forth, and she did nothing to try to stop them.

They'd arrived too late—for Ledge, at least. She'd killed him.

Chapter 41

The EMTs had left the crime scene with a beaten and devastated Liza McAllister. Deputy Lewis was sent to follow and stay stationed by the victim. They needed some answers, but she was in no condition to offer any coherent responses.

The search of the car parked in the garage produced an unaddressed, sealed, white envelope above the driver's visor. Hannah pulled his pocket knife from his pocket. With gloved hands, he methodically opened the mysterious envelope. One sheet of paper was in there. He pulled it out. Reyes snapped photos as he proceeded.

Scribbled in what he could only assume was Ledge McAllister's handwriting was a quick and direct note addressed to:

To Whom It May Concern:

If you're reading this, I failed my children. Please let them know I tried. And I'm sorry they're now alone.

Ledge

Silence surrounded Hannah as he returned the letter to the envelope and placed it on the seat of the car for the crew to bag and tag when they arrived.

"Murder? Suicide?" Ross asked with a puzzled look on his face.

Hannah shrugged. "That guy was fishing in the ocean without a ship."

"Undoubtedly so." Ross agreed, turning away from the car.

Reyes was diligently snapping more crime scene photos inside the barn along with another agent. Hannah had exited the building and turned to face the house. He drew in a fortifying breath of fresh air. Death was always a rank scent. He had vaguely deduced what had happened in the barn, but he needed Liza to be well enough to fill in the missing pieces. They had heard Ledge terrorizing her as they flanked the barn and house. The devastation in the barn was a chaotic disaster. The target had clearly lost his mind. And had the outcome not been what it was, there would have been two bodies on the scene.

Now they needed to check the house, another part of the entire puzzle surrounding this abduction. Hannah hoped the house provided more clues to the perp's insanity, for the sake of Liza McAllister.

"Ready to check the house?" Sheriff Ross asked.

"Let's do it," Hannah said as he turned around to holler at Reyes to come with them so he could record the scene in the house. Reyes rushed out of the barn, leaving the other agent to finish documenting the area.

SWAT had descended in two teams upon the house and the barn at the same time. They had cleared both buildings—no one else was around except the two McAllisters. Now, Reyes swapped out the SD card in the camera for a fresh one. He started snapping photos again as they neared the house. The door had been found open when they arrived on the scene.

Entering the house behind Reyes, it smelled as if it had been recently cleaned and dusted. Hannah noticed the outdated feel of the house—until they entered the kitchen. This was the room that Handyman Bill had mentioned assisting Mr. McAllister with. Not much to be found in this Spic-n-Span environment, aside from a crumpled water bottle lying on the kitchen tile floor near the trash bin. They silently walked throughout the rest of the main rooms, listening to the snapping camera as Reyes clicked away. So far, nothing much to see. All the rooms were clean and tidy. No papers lying about; drawers and cupboards were eerily organized. Everything was in its place. Labels faced forward in the pantry, lined up like soldiers in a row. It made Hannah's teeth itch.

Hannah and Ross were standing just inside one of the bedrooms, waiting for Reyes to finish photographing the room. Hannah noted the PJs lying haphazardly on the floor and the disheveled sheets. Reyes had opened the dresser drawers, and the clothes appeared to be that of a man. Mr. McAllister's, he presumed. They had found Ms. McAllister's clothing in the bathroom cupboard—an odd location, to be sure. Hannah shook his head at the strangeness of this case. Then Reyes poked his head out of the closet.

"Hannah, you need to see this," Reyes said as he nodded his head toward the closet and then disappeared.

Hannah and Ross followed. Inside the closet was another door. Hannah shook his head and sighed. *The plot thickens.*

He stepped into what was essentially a secret room, Ross right behind him.

"This is interesting," was all Hannah could think to say.

"Thought you'd like it." Reyes had a smile on his face. "Over here, I found this cell phone and cord, along with this folder and possibly a journal. These are the only few things that don't look as if they've been here forever."

Hannah reached for the cell phone first and saw it was either turned off or dead. He pushed in the power button and watched the screen come to life. After a few seconds, he was thankful to discover it was unlocked. When he slid his finger across the screen, Ms. McAllister's picture was the background image, smiling back at him. She was in a Midland High School cheerleader uniform, just a teenager. Her wide smile lit up her entire face.

Hannah clicked on the phone to check the last number dialed. It was to Lawson McAllister, the son. The other calls also matched the reports from the phone company. He closed out of that and went to the internet browser to see if the history was still there. The only thing that showed was the drug Ledge must have used on his ex-wife in order to abduct her. He showed the screen to Reyes, who snapped a photo of it.

"Check this out." Ross handed the folder to Hannah.

Hannah saw the drawings of a beautiful kitchen that somewhat matched the kitchen here. The placement was a bit different, but Hannah recalled the kitchen at the suspect's home, and the layout on these pages would have matched the layout of the kitchen space there. He flipped through and saw handwritten notes. He wondered who had drawn these.

Next, Ross handed the small journal to him. Hannah saw more notes that were more scribbled than flowing.

"Check the page that has the ribbon marker," Ross said.

Hannah found the green ribbon barely hanging out from the bottom of the small book and opened it.

He read it out loud: *"She's mine. I have her now, and she's mine."* He looked up at his fellow officers. "Christ Almighty," he said, then went back to flipping through the pages.

"I'm done in here," Reyes said as he exited the closet to photograph the rest of the rooms they hadn't been in yet.

Hannah nodded and continued to peruse the journal looking for any more clues to the state of mind of the perp. The writing appeared to have started about the time Liza had left Ledge. He noted the date she left, the date of their day in court, and the date of their anniversary. Hannah read on and found that Ledge had stalked her almost the entire time they were apart. He even made mention of one night he was able to gain entrance into her new place.

"Ross, listen to this." He read: *"She must have wanted me to be with her tonight. She left the door unlocked, and I slipped in. She was asleep like an angel. Her hair was spilled over her pillow, and I stroked it. She didn't wake, but I got to see her sleep again."* He looked up from the pages and arched his brows.

"Well, that's not creepy at all." Ross rolled his eyes.

"Here is why we didn't find forced entry to her home. He went that night and put a new lock on the back door."

Ross shook his head. "Dude's nuts, man."

Hannah read on and found the plan McAllister had hatched to take her away to his grandparents' home. He looked at the date of the writing: September 2nd.

"He details the plan to get her back. As if kidnapping her will make her see the *error* of her ways. Jesus." Hannah read on, sometimes stumbling over the words, they were written so illegibly. As if the guy had been rushed. *Or manic.* "He wrote about how she'd tried to escape, but he fixed it so she'd never be able to leave without him. That's the last of it. It ends there."

He put the notebook back on the cabinet, knowing he couldn't take it with him. The folks from the crime lab still had their jobs to do.

Time to go to the hospital and speak with the victim.

Chapter 42

Friday

Detective Hannah arrived at the West Branch Medical Center around 12:30 a.m., where he was directed to Ms. McAllister's room by an ER nurse. He found Deputy Lewis standing outside the room.

"Detective Hannah. She's currently resting, but I'll update you on her medical status." He pulled out his notebook to go over the details.

Hannah nodded and waited for Lewis to fill him in. Ms. McAllister's room was stationed at the end of an empty hall. Hannah assumed the staff had positioned her there to ward off curious lookie-loos, given Lewis's presence. No one was within earshot, but they spoke quietly anyway.

"X-rays came back clean on her ankle and her ribs. Her left foot is badly bruised. She has quite a few busies on her person, in fact. Her face, neck, ribs, a few on her legs. Her hand has a small cut that has already started to heal. The cut on her forehead has scabbed over. I didn't get a chance to speak with her before the pain pills they gave her knocked her out. I haven't heard a peep from her room. Hers is an interior room that has no windows, so the only way out is through this door that I'm standing in front of." Lewis drew himself up taller—as if that were possible since he had been standing at attention the entire time of his recount.

Hannah had to try hard to hide his smirk. The deputy was nice enough, but a little on the stiff side. "Did she say anything to the EMTs on the way to the hospital, or maybe to the medical staff?"

"I spoke with EMTs Stevens and Rogers when I arrived behind them, and they had already passed her off to the medical team. They said she was out most of the ride, but her vitals remained stable. She moaned when they hit bumps in the road. And Stevens remembers her saying that she didn't mean to do it. That's all they had. I've been here with her, and she's said nothing except an occasional response for the medical staff attending to her. And they only asked her about where she hurt, how much did it hurt. As you probably noticed, they were swamped down there tonight. Must be the full moon."

"Okay. How long has she been out?"

"About thirty minutes."

"Let's see if we can rouse her a bit and get a statement." Hannah knocked on the door and walked in. "Ms. McAllister?"

She opened her eyes slowly and winced. The light from the hall was bright, and she shielded her eyes. "Yes?"

Lewis closed the door behind Hannah and stayed stationed outside. The nursing staff had the light above her bed turned down to a pale nightlight.

"Ms. McAllister, I'm Detective Sergeant Hannah from Midland Police Department. We've been trying to find you. Are you well enough to speak with me right now?"

"Yes. I'm better, thank you." She tried to raise herself up in the bed but stopped and gritted her teeth. Hannah handed her the bed controller that had slid off the side of the bed.

"Thank you." She clicked on the button to raise the head of the bed. She grimaced as the bed moved. Hannah waited patiently as she settled herself, turning the overhead light up a bit and blinking hard a few times after she did so. She said, "Please sit down. I'd feel better if you did."

Hannah sat in the chair next to the bed and clasped his hands together. "Ms. McAllister," he began.

"Please, call me Liza."

Hannah smiled at her. "Liza, please, if you could start from the beginning and finish with where we found you."

"I will, but I need to know if my kids have been called. Are they okay? I ... the nurses asked me if I needed to contact anyone, and I ... I didn't want them to see me like this. And I ... I don't know how to tell them that ... that their father ..." She sobbed through her words. "That I killed their father."

The tears broke, and Hannah reached for the box of tissues on the rolling table at the end of her bed. She took them, her hand shaking, and tried to compose herself. Hannah waited. It was then he noticed the shiny object on her left ring finger. A wedding ring. *Odd.* Mr. McAllister was sporting one as well when they had viewed his body. Hannah filed that away for a little later.

"Sorry, I've never done anything like this before. I need to start there. It was me that kicked him, to keep him away from me, and he lost his balance and fell through the railing. I couldn't reach him in time to stop him from falling. I saw it. I saw his face. I couldn't help him." The words rushed out of her this time, the stammering gone in her apparent need to get it all out. Then she started bawling again, and Hannah did not interrupt. After several minutes, she finally was able to breathe regularly and look him in the eye.

"Am I going to jail? I am, aren't I?"

"Ma'am, we're trying to get the facts. Please, start back at the beginning. Tell me everything you can remember."

Liza took a deep breath and thought back to the day this all had started. Saturday morning. "I had a cruise I was supposed to go on ..." and she began to tell the story, starting from the day she was taken. Hannah sat quietly, ready to take notes on the pad he had pulled out of his breast pocket, listening intently.

"I was up and all ready to leave on the cruise. I had my luggage in the truck already and had walked out of the bathroom, heading toward the kitchen to get my purse and phone."

Liza stopped and appeared to be thinking.

"Take your time. What do you remember next?"

"It's blurry, I remember hearing a noise and ..." She laid her head back against the pillow and put her hand on her forehead. She rested for a minute with her eyes closed. Hannah made no movement and said nothing.

Finally, Liza's eyes shot open.

"It was Ledge! He was in the kitchen. He was standing by the back door in the kitchen with his hand on the doorknob. I freaked. I ran toward the garage, and then I went down. Something knocked me over. I remember hearing glass breaking. I think it was the glass pitcher on the table near the living room." She stopped and looked at her right hand, running a finger over the cut that was healing there. She looked up at him, "I tried to get up. That must have been when I cut my hand. I don't remember anything after that until I woke up in that orange room." She stopped again, taking time to collect herself. "I don't know how he got in my house. I always left the door locked and always checked the doors twice before I went to bed. I didn't even keep a spare key lying around." She shook her head and immediately winced from the effort. She put her hands to her temples and closed her eyes.

"Liza, would you like some water?"

"Yes, please." She didn't look up.

Hannah got up, reached over to get the cup on the cart at the end of her bed, and handed it to her.

"Thank you."

"You're welcome. Again, please take your time." He smiled at her to reassure her that he was in no hurry.

Chapter 43

Hannah allowed Liza the time she needed to recall the events of her abduction. She seemed honest and forthright in the retelling of the events that led her to last night's tragedy. She lamented that it was a tragedy in the sense that the man who died had been a good man at one time. Hannah watched as she absently twisted the wedding ring on her finger. She stopped as soon as she saw where his eyes had landed. She hadn't mentioned the ring and why it was still on her hand.

She was on the verge of tears again when she took the ring off and handed it to Hannah. "You'll probably need this. I ... he ..." She struggled to explain. "He half proposed to me, half forced it back on my hand. I acquiesced and put it back on to keep, you know ... the Demon at bay. That is until he went nuts when it had fallen off the first time I tried to escape. Of course, he found it and put it back on. I can't seem to get rid of this evil talisman."

He took the ring and placed it into a clean zipper bag he always kept in his pocket. *Never know when you need to bag evidence.*

"Am I under arrest?" Liza asked quietly as she twisted the blanket in her lap. "Are you going to tell the kids I killed him?" She looked at him as if she were ready to be hauled off to prison in chains.

"Liza, I will leave that up to you to tell your children about your ex-husband. Unless you'd rather I tell them?" Hannah stoically looked at her, not giving anything away as to his thoughts. He saw nothing in the evidence they had collected so far that pointed to any wrongdoing on her part. *Self-defense.*

"No. I ... I can do it. Thank you."

Hannah nodded. "I have your statement. Of course, we'll verify the information. If everything holds true, then this will be deemed an accident.

I'm certain your kids will give you a ride home, but if not, here's my card. I'll make sure someone gets you there safely." He set the card on the rolling table and left as Liza continued clutching the blanket in her hands, twisting it nervously.

***

Detective Hannah left Deputy Lewis to keep watch over Liza until her kids arrived. He got back to his car and dialed Lawson McAllister before he left the parking lot. He wanted his full concentration on the call before he drove back to the crime scene. Hannah cleared his throat as an extremely tired-sounding Lawson answered the phone.

"Hello?"

"Lawson McAllister, this is Detective Hannah. We found your mom. She's okay."

"Oh my …thank you! Can we see her?" Lawson's voice boomed through the receiver. He was awake now.

"You're welcome. Yes, you can see her. She had an accident, but she's okay. She's at the West Branch Medical Center." Hannah could hear crying in the background and assumed it was the sister.

"What? What kind of accident?" Lawson asked.

"She can explain that all to you when you get there. She's resting right now, but she'll be waiting for you. Again, she's fine."

"Okay, okay. What's the address?"

"I'll give you that. Do you have anyone who can drive you? I would rather you didn't drive yourselves."

"Yes, we're at Aunt Trinity's." Lawson paused. "Are you sure she's all right?"

"She's fine. But she's missing you guys."

"And… what about Dad?" Lawson cautiously asked.

"That's a question that will be answered when you see your mom." Hannah left it at that, not wanting to make an anxious ride up north worse.

"Thank you detective." Lawson said, and hung up.

Epilogue

Liza slipped out of the house onto the cold patio to get some fresh air and clear her head for a few minutes. Her feet crunched on the early snow that had arrived ahead of the kid's birthday and decided to stick around. It'd been over a month since they laid Ledge in his grave. The twins hadn't left her side, doting on her like she was a baby bird. She was physically healing well as far as the doctor was concerned. She was out of the brace they'd put her ankle in. Her heart and head … well, they were another story.

She sighed and watched her breath travel toward the patio window as she looked past the mist at the group that was gathered in her dining room. They were her rocks. Everyone had come together to wish the twins a happy twentieth birthday today. Everyone, that is, except their father.

Tears threatened again for the umpteenth time that day.

She turned away from the happy scene as her thoughts traveled back to that dreadful day. Thankfully, Lexi and Lawson hadn't blamed her or held a grudge for Ledge's fateful fall. They had seen him lose control with her a few times before, but they had never seen him capricious. Liza was grateful for that small blessing. Ledge had loved their children with all his heart, and she hated that it had ended the way it had.

But she was damn happy to be alive.

Arms swooped in and wrapped themselves around her. Trinity's arms were like a bear trap around her shoulders, and Chrissie was there to complete the comforting hug Liza hadn't realized she'd needed. The trio stood silently still for several minutes before Chrissie started shaking from the cold.

"You've become a Southerner." Liza broke the silence with a quick critique of Chrissie's new job and hotter weather she now lived in.

"I might not be able to stand the snow, but it's still be-au-tiful," Chrissie said through chattering teeth.

"Let's go in before you freeze to death," Trinity said, then winced at her words with a peek at Liza.

"I'm okay. Really, I am. Thank you both for your help. You gals have been so good to me I don't know how to thank you." Liza sniffed and brushed at her tears as they started to walk back into the house.

"We're gl-ad you'rrre s-s-safe now," Chrissie said, her chattering worse.

The loud conversation in the room swallowed any response Liza had as they entered the room one by one. Trinity closed the sliding glass door behind her as she moved Liza toward the party. It was time for the kids to cut the cake and make their yearly wish. Liza knew they were getting too old for parties but was thankful for their initiative to keep her spirits bolstered this year.

Everyone started singing "Happy Birthday" to the twins as Liza brought the cake out, candles blazing. She smiled at them as best she could for indulging her with the party. Chrissie's voice was drowning out everyone else so that she almost didn't notice Trinity's off-key rendition.

"Make a wish!" Ollie said. He looked at Liza with a knowing look. Ollie had apologized over and over about Ledge. But Liza wasn't having it. It was what it was. Ledge was responsible for his own actions on the day he died and before that, even. And she was trying hard to believe every word of it. Every. Single. Day.

She struggled with the image of him lying dead on the barn floor, broken. Almost every night, she woke up drenched in sweat, screaming his name. Sometimes, it was about the night he'd gone over the ledge. Although more recently, her nightmares had turned more sinister. This morning, around 3:00 a.m., she woke up choking and coughing, grasping her throat. She had been trapped under his weight, and his long fingers wrapped around her neck. There was black coal where Ledge's eyes had been, and he was laughing as she gasped for air. "You will never leave me. You don't get to leave me. You are mine forever!"

Liza shivered from the memory of the night terror.

"One day at a time," her therapist had told her. She started seeing one a few weeks ago. She had finally stopped crying all the time. The kids helped her with that, mostly due to their being *helicopter parents*. Liza was making due. She had to. Smiling at the kids after they blew out all the candles, the smoke alarm went off. Everyone started laughing, and someone grabbed a kitchen towel to fan the alarm, breaking the spell.

"*Lizabeth.*"

Liza jumped and squelched a scream with her hand on her mouth and one on her heart. Larry, Ledge's attorney—actually, her attorney, too—stood with his hands up, as if startled at her reaction. Liza never wanted to hear that name again. She politely smiled at Larry, and he held out his arms to give her a hug. She accepted and then quickly stepped back.

"I didn't mean to startle you. Is now a bad time?" Larry quietly asked.

"No, not at all. Let's get this over with." Liza smiled back at Larry, who handed her the kids' birthday gift.

Liza didn't say a word as she gave the large envelope to Lexi and Lawson. They were old enough to know what Ledge's wishes were should he pass. Lawson allowed Lexi to do the honors as he watched. Upon reading the papers she'd pulled out, they both looked up at Liza and then Larry. Liza smiled sadly, and then Larry said, "Your dad wanted you both to have his agency. It's in your names, but you won't receive managing ownership until you graduate and have been trained in all aspects of the business."

"That is, if you both want it?" Liza added.

The twins looked at each other and then went to their mother to give her a hug.

"We'll try to make Dad proud," Lexi said in a tearful whisper.

"You two always made him proud." Liza wiped the tears away from her sweet daughter's face, while she reined in her own. "Now, let's cut that cake."

The party went on for hours. Life went on.

One day at a time. Her new mantra.

~~ Acknowledgments ~~

I want to lay a Gargantuan Bouquet of Gratitude in the hands of the following people who helped make all this possible!

- ➢ **Chris James** - Stupendous Wealth of Crime Help - Thank you for answering my daunting questions! I appreciate your help and hope I did it justice. I also pray I didn't embarrass you for anything I may have misunderstood. <3

- ➢ **Janet Fix** - Fantabulous Editor - Thank you for enduring my questions, my boring written words, and pushing me to write better than I have in a long time. We made it to 2020!! <3 thewordverve.com

- ➢ **Bob Houston** – Life Saver of a Formatter – Thank you Bob for coming to my rescue to get this ready! I appreciate it more than words can say! http:// facebook.com/ eBook Formatting/info

- ➢ **Joshua Jadon** - Chillacious Cover Creator - Thank you Joshua for putting this great cover together! I love it! <3

- ➢ **BJ Holwerda** - Beautimous Barn Photo with Bonus Ghost Story. I'm pretty sure that the ghost is the reason that barn is no longer there. ;-) <3
  You can find his amazing photos on Instagram: bjholwerda

***

I wholeheartedly thank each and every author (below in alphabetical order), who gave me some insight, answered my questions through the years, and quite frankly put up with me when I repeatedly pestered them; lurked in the shadows, and watched them work. I admit I wore them down. ;-) If I missed anyone here, my sincere apologies! Much love you to all! <3

- ➢ **Kathy Bennett** (A Deadly Prayer, first in the series, and more)
- ➢ **Rebecca Forster** (Hostile Witness, first in the series, and more)
- ➢ **J. A. Huss** (Rook & Ronin, first in the series, and more)
- ➢ **Bonnie R. Paulson** (Broken Trails, first in the series, and more)
- ➢ **Kennedy Layne** (Captured Innocence, first in the series, and more)
- ➢ **John Locke** (Lethal People, first in the series, and more)
- ➢ **Kallypso Masters** (Jessie's Hideout, first in the series, and more)
- ➢ **Rick Murcer** (Caribbean Moon, first in the series, and more)

Pick up their books; they're great reads in their genre! <3

~~*Family & Friends*~~

To My Handsome Husband, My Heart, My World,
Thank you for putting up with my long writing hours to get this thing published. There are no words to describe how much that means to me. I'm thankful I picked you to finish life with. I love you more! <3 <3

***

To My Parents,
You gave me and my siblings a wonderful life! You are both amazing people, and I'm so proud to call you Mom and Dad. Thank you is not enough to tell you how grateful I am for the opportunity to be one of your children. Love you more than you know! <3 <3

***

To My Siblings,

You are both wonderful! I love you both more than you realize, and I am thankful for having you in my life! Thank you for your encouragement! You guys have both made some great choices in your life! Keep up the great work! I'm proud of you! <3 <3

***

To My Second Parents,

Thank you for accepting me into your family. You are both dear to me and loved! I am so glad I married your son and got to be a part of your lives. <3 <3

***

To My Dear Friend,

Thank you for reading through some chapters for me. I appreciate your insight and encouraging words. I'm blessed to still have you in my life. Love you! <3 <3

***

And last but never least,

THANK YOU to YOU for reading my first novel! I appreciate you taking the time to read this far, and I pray you have a blessed day. <3 <3

Please drop a review at your place of purchase, or on https://www.goodreads.com/.

Please follow me if you are up for some fun things coming in relation to this book and others to come (see links below).

Blessings to you all,
Fallon

***

If you enjoyed this story, please sign up for my newsletter to receive notification of my next release—no excess emails, only releases, I value my inbox as I'm sure you do! ☺

Newsletter Signup:

https://www.fallonraynes.com/contact-me

Want more than just a notice about the next release? I also have a group page if you're interested in joining please follow the link below. Group members will have opportunities to get in on book details, games, and learn about new Fallon fun things to come. ☺

"Escape From Reality" group:

https://www.facebook.com/groups/705411259864839/

Follow Me If You Dare:

- Facebook: https://www.facebook.com/FallonRaynesAuthor/
- Instagram: https://www.instagram.com/fallonraynesofficial/
- Twitter: https://twitter.com/FallonRaynes
- Pinterest: https://www.pinterest.com/fallonraynes/
- Goodreads: https://www.goodreads.com/user/show/109722588-fallon-raynes

~~~AFTER THE STORY~~~

Q: What is After The Story (ATS)?

A: It's a wrap up after the story, my version of an Author's Note.

What you May or May Not find in this section:

Errors: Grammatical or otherwise. It's like a journal entry for me so the editor doesn't see this section. #notsorry. You may find my thoughts about the book, my fanciful ramblings, inspiration, gratitude, what's next, author links, possible giveaways, and maybe a mystery.

I follow an author (I'll mention her later) that I love to read and she does this end of book thing that I ABSOLUTELY LOVE, especially when I listen to her audible books. She tapes her version of the "Author's Note" herself, and it makes me feel satisfied after reading/listening to her books. When I first listened to that cold abrupt ending "This is Audible" on some other books (different authors), and there was nothing else at the end of that book, except maybe a few notes about the production, I felt dumped. LOL

It was then that I realized I wanted to do this for my readers. I felt like it was an easier transition at the end to close the book and say a few words. So, I reached out to her and asked her if she minded if I emulated hers with my own spin. Being the Awesome person she is, she was cool with it. So, I hope you all feel that little bit of closure after you read this. :-)

~~~~~
~~~~~

First:

I hope you enjoyed *Dangerous Ledges*. I'm so excited to be putting THE END on my first published novel. It was a long and winding road to get here, but a learning adventure nonetheless! I'm excited to hear your feedback. IF you thoroughly hated it, tell me why. And I don't mean just say "It Sucked", Or "I hated the cover so I gave you 1 star". I want to know why it sucked for you. Seriously.

If you loved it, why did you love it? Please drop a review at your purchase site, and/or on GoodReads.com. IF you are not familiar with Good Reads, it is a great site to find new books and authors. Similar to an index file you'd find at a library, only filled with reviews. :-)

I had a beginning and an end for Dangerous Ledges when the book popped in my head. I just needed to fill in the middle, and these characters kept changing the rules on me. So editing this after my editor had it the first go round took me some time. I had a few health things thrown in the mix, the day job sucked the life out of me again (my creativity was Zilch during those periods), but I was finally able to wrap it up, and finish it in 2019. I cannot put into words how I feel about my first published novel being in your hands.

Ledge:

Where do I start? He was always a dark figure in my mind as soon as I saw him. He had an edge to him. He was sexy, and intelligent, and got sucked into a raw deal with the drug he was on. Sadly he didn't get off that drug in time to save his sanity. He truly was a good guy at heart and loved his Lizabeth, his angel. But that Demon; he really ruined things.

My two cents: I think if you're taking a drug, and it is making you feel depressed or crazy, please stop taking it, and get to your doctor. IF you are not feeling like you are in "good hands", Please, FIND A NEW DOCTOR! It is allowed. And please take heed when your "person" tells you, that you are not right, or need help. I know mental health is not easy to wade through, but when you have someone in your corner listen to them.

Depression can suck you in and never spit you out. So please seek help if you're feeling stuck. *gets of soap box*

Liza:

She was a short, petite, little thing, full of energy and fire. She was a fixer of things, would stand up for herself and others, and of course intelligent. She always had a smile on her face in my mind. Well, except during most of this book. ;-) She loved her kids, loved her girls and had a zest for life until Ledge's demon took that from her. I'm sure she'll find that smile again someday.

Story:

Those two characters surprised the hell out of me. The ebb and flow of their attraction toward each other confused me sometimes. It's like WHY are you there Liza, RUN! But, her heartstrings were attached from the years of the love she once knew and she kept falling back into old habits with him. She forced me to see that "before" life of theirs.

IF you are in a bad relationship, that is toxic, verbal, violent, Please, find a better life for yourself. I know it's not easy, but I implore you to leave it, and move on. IF one person is not happy, you both won't be. *slides soap box firmly out of the way*

I will admit, I cried when Ledge died, but his death was unavoidable. It broke my heart to write that scene, but that's where the story led. I don't think there would have been a better closure; his mind was too far gone.

Will there be an "After" for Liza?

I don't know. I can't say any of Liza's crew won't show up later. It depends on what story crosses my mind, and at what time. I am doubtful I'll write a romance book, but I won't rule anything out.

Follow me to catch future giveaways and fun stuff.
Facebook: https://www.facebook.com/FallonRaynesAuthor/

Instagram: https://www.instagram.com/fallonraynesofficial/
Twitter: https://twitter.com/FallonRaynes
Website: https://www.fallonraynes.com/

~~~~~

Second

I'm going to give a HUGE shout out of love to author JA Huss. IF you're a fan of HEA (Happily Ever After), naughty HEA, and some Fantasy HEA, that can be dark and twisty, RUN to your book dealer and get you some. I FAN girl all over that poor woman and she still allows me to stalk her, I mean follow her. ;-) What can I say, I love the dark twisty turns, and I don't write HEA, but I do love to read it, and she is a Master at it! :-)

Gratitude

Thank you to all the people who keep our Country and Communities safe. May God bless you and keep you safe while you do your jobs! You are appreciated! <3

Thoughts

- Love: If you go to bed angry, you have tomorrow to make it better. Life sucks sometimes, but each day brings a new opportunity. Don't let your pride get in your way. Pick Your Battles.

- Family: I love them! They are the best thing that God has given me! <3

Wrap Up

Sign up here for my newsletter at my website:
https://www.fallonraynes.com/contact-me.

I am not a person that likes a ton of emails, so you won't get that many from me. I plan to keep that only for book releases. My blog posts won't be many either. I'd rather spend time putting words on the pages.
~~~~~

But, if you want to stay updated on a regular basis, follow me on Facebook. IF you really want to be included in special things that I will share with my fans, please join my Facebook Fan Group. I plan to have some fun in there and maybe ask questions that might be included in a future book. ☺ https://www.facebook.com/groups/705411259864839/

Thank you for sticking around and reading my first ATS! I appreciate you! ☺

The Applicant will be the next release, with more on that later. Until next time, Blessings to you and yours! <3

Fallon

About The Author

Fallon Raynes is a paper pusher by day, writer by night. Writing has been in Fallon's blood for as long as she can remember. Short stories and poems kept her mind at ease earlier on. Life's adventures have swirled in her mind to create some exaggerated stories that she's excited to put to paper and share with the world. To relax, Fallon enjoys watching the ID and Hallmark channels, reading, and the outdoors.

Fallon resides in lower Michigan with her husband and fur-baby.

- Website: https://www.fallonraynes.com/
- Facebook: https://www.facebook.com/FallonRaynesAuthor/
- Facebook Group: https://www.facebook.com/groups/705411259864839/
- Instagram: https://www.instagram.com/fallonraynesofficial/
- Twitter: https://twitter.com/FallonRaynes
- Website: https://www.fallonraynes.com/